THE CONTEST

A Gutsy Girl Book

The Contest

CAROLINE STELLINGS

Second Story Press

Library and Archives Canada Cataloguing in Publication

Stellings, Caroline, 1961-
The contest / by Caroline Stellings.

(The gutsy girl series)
ISBN 978-1-897187-64-7

I. Title. II. Series: Gutsy girl series

PS8587.T4448C66 2009   jC813'.6   C2009-903077-2

Edited by Anne Millyard
Designed by Melissa Kaita
Cover by Gillian Newland

Printed and bound in Canada

Mixed Sources
Product group from well-managed
forests, controlled sources and
recycled wood or fibre
FSC www.fsc.org Cert no. SW-COC-000952
© 1996 Forest Stewardship Council

*Second Story Press gratefully acknowledges the support of the Ontario Arts Council
and the Canada Council for the Arts for our publishing program. We acknowledge
the financial support of the Government of Canada through the Book
Publishing Industry Development Program.*

ONTARIO ARTS COUNCIL
CONSEIL DES ARTS DE L'ONTARIO

Canada Council   Conseil des Arts
for the Arts   du Canada

Published by
SECOND STORY PRESS
20 Maud Street, Suite 401
Toronto, ON M5V 2M5
www.secondstorypress.ca

Printed on Rolland Enviro100, which contains
100% recycled post-consumer fibre, is EcoLogo,
Processed Chlorine Free and FSC Recycled
certified and manufactured using biogas energy.

For Aunts Opal, Ena, and Florence, and Uncle William Bate.

We are all in the gutter,
but some of us are looking at the stars.

– Oscar Wilde, *Lady Windermere's Fan*

Chapter 1

Rosy made her daily trip to the Barton Street branch of the Hamilton Public Library, imagining she was near the ocean, not the toxic soup called Hamilton Bay. The black fumes that spewed out of the city's steel mills choked her. The cars roaring by choked her. The humidity choked her. She clenched her fists when the exhaust from an idling pickup truck choked her.

Rosy's only escape from the city's north end was the library. She could breathe in there, thanks to the air conditioner, which helped ease the symptoms of her asthma. And she could make her getaway to the salt air and red sands of Prince Edward Island. The land of potatoes and Anne.

Rosy was almost twelve – would be on the twenty-second of August – and had already devoured every book Lucy Maud Montgomery had written. Helen, the librarian at Barton, ordered a new copy of *Anne of Green Gables* for the branch because the one there had thirty-seven pages missing. She let Rosy keep the discarded copy.

Rosy was glad to finally *own* a book, even with the missing pages, but what she really wanted was a boxed set of the whole series of *Anne* books – factory sealed and fresh off the press, with the smell of printer's ink still on them. The complete set of eight, never before read by anyone else. Never touched by anyone else. Not sneezed on, not set down on a bus seat, not dropped on the sidewalk. She would open each one carefully, then write on the inside cover, neatly and with a green felt pen: "This book belongs to Rosy Taylor."

Helen said she could order all of Lucy Maud Montgomery's books listed in the public library system. There were almost two hundred listings, but some were videos and DVDs, and Rosy didn't have a television, let alone a VCR or DVD player. She told Helen a person's imagination was better anyhow.

Rosy's mother couldn't afford anything more than the food on the table and the roof over their heads. She washed floors at the Saver-Mart supermarket, and took as many night shifts as she could so her kids didn't have to rely on the food bank. Even when they had to, they only took macaroni and cheese dinner and maybe some powdered milk and canned peas. Rosy had three older brothers – Ben was seventeen, Patrick was fifteen (he had asthma too) and John was thirteen – and they all ate an awful lot. Hence, the food bank.

Rosy's mother was Native Canadian and had grown up on the Six Nations reserve near Brantford. She was named *Jis-go-ga*, which means Robin, because she was born on the first day of spring. Rosy told her that made her an Aries and it meant she was adventurous and brave. It meant nothing could bring her down. Rosy was glad to be half Mohawk. She just *knew* it made her fascinating.

As Ben was seventeen, he stayed with the other kids while their mother worked. He studied constantly. His dream was to have a career in medicine one day, but he didn't have a snowball's chance in the steel factory's blast furnace of ever affording university.

They didn't have a father. He had left when Robin was pregnant with Rosy – he went to the beer store and never came back. James Taylor – also known as Taylor James, Jimmy Bing, and Bing Taylor – was of Irish and English descent. He spent half his life in the poolroom on King Street and the other half in the Hamilton Detention Center. He met Robin when she was eighteen and was taken by her long black hair. He told her he'd worship her forever and they got married thirteen days after that. He started pushing her around the next Tuesday. Someone said he ended up in Reno, Nevada.

But Rosy's mom wasn't the kind to go around complaining. She didn't call him a no-good bum or a heap of trash. She threw out his picture, along with his ashtrays, and put his clothes in the Salvation Army bin. Then she went to work and never mentioned his name again. (Rosy told her she was able to do this because she was an Aries.) And when men started gathering around, asking Robin out on dates and telling her she was gorgeous, she refused them all. She hadn't even had a coffee with a man since the day Rosy's father walked out the door. Except for Jay and Sebastian next door. She still has coffee with them.

Rosy figured that although Anne of Green Gables was an orphan, it was a fair trade for getting to live on an unpolluted island with the ocean and a haunted wood at her door, rather than in a rental house on a dead-end street in Hamilton.

It was really only half a house – divided down the middle so the landlord could get double the rent. The other half had seen many residents over the years, including an enterprising Italian couple who grew grapes, tomatoes, and eggplants in a backyard the size of a postage stamp.

Jay and Sebastian had moved in the previous summer. Jay wanted to be near Robin, since it was his cousin who had left her in the lurch. He and Sebastian were professional hairdressers. They worked at a salon in Hamilton, The Tangerine Coiffure, where the price of a single haircut could feed Rosy's family for a week. Jay and Sebastian were saving money to start their own salon, and it was going to be called Jay Sebastian, and it was going to be the best one in the whole Golden Horseshoe.

No one on Rosy's street – no one in the entire north end – could afford The Tangerine, but Jay and Sebastian did the neighbors' hair at their home on the barter system. Mrs. Rodrigues traded two loaves of Portuguese sweet bread and a macaroni casserole for a wash and set and cleaned their place whenever her hair needed coloring. Mr. and Mrs. Wing, who ran The Golden Leaf Chinese take-out, had their hair trimmed once a month in exchange for the Number 7 Special: plain fried rice, sweet and sour shrimp, mixed vegetables, vegetable chow mein, and fortune cookies. Like Rosy and her mother, Jay and Sebastian were vegetarians, but they would eat shrimp. (Just not anything that blinks.)

Rosy's brothers shared a small room behind the kitchen. It was so heaped up with sports equipment that they didn't have space to move. (All of it came from thrift shops. Rosy said that at her place even the sweat was secondhand.) Ben and John were exceptional athletes. Patrick couldn't play endurance sports like soccer, but baseball was okay. Rosy couldn't participate much at all.

Rosy had her own room upstairs. It was hot in the summer and the wind blew through the cracks, but it had a window so she could see the stars.

Chapter 2

Rosy ran up the steps to the door of the library and peered through the glass to see the clock on the wall. It was almost ten, and Helen was unlocking the door with a grin on her face. Helen was one of those people who smiled even when she was angry. (Rosy only saw her get mad once: when a kid stuck his gum in a *Harry Potter* book to mark his place.) She called everyone "dear" and "honey" and smelled like menthol.

Rosy had a keen sense of smell in spite of, or perhaps because of, her asthma. She figured if her plans to become a stage actress didn't pan out, she could always get a job with the police, sniffing out drugs.

"Come on in, honey!" Helen released the lock and

pushed open the heavy door. "*The Story Girl* is here for you. I think you're going to enjoy this book," she added, handing it to Rosy.

"Thanks, Helen," gasped Rosy, out of breath from running too fast.

"You okay?" Helen knew Rosy had asthma. "You shouldn't be running in this heat! It's ninety-five in the shade."

What shade? Rosy asked herself. The trees in the city were dismal things, spindly and yellow, and any leaves that dared to form in May – that dared to believe they had a future – soon gave up and dropped off onto the sidewalk only to be washed by dirty rain into a sewer.

"I'm good now, thanks." Rosy pulled her chair in to the table and starting reading.

"How does it look so far, dear?"

Rosy hadn't even made it through the first sentence, for Pete's sake! Helen was obviously anxious about something.

When Helen sat down beside her, Rosy noticed Helen smelled more like bananas than menthol. "You know *The Story Girl* was sent from Rockton branch? Well, they sent this, too." She stuck a flyer in Rosy's hand.

Rosy took a minute to read it. Helen expected her to jump out of the chair or something, but Rosy sat there, motionless, staring at the piece of green paper. Finally, she read it aloud.

"Westfield Heritage Village, Rockton Ontario, is pleased to announce that this year's Anne of Green Gables look-alike contest will be held on Sunday, September 1st. First prize is a boxed set of all eight books in the Anne series, by L. M. Montgomery, and a sterling silver trophy, to be engraved with the winner's name. This is part of our annual Anne of Green Gables Day. Please post the following schedule at your branch."

It went on to describe the different events: a tea party, an Avonlea road race, a parade, and – of course – the Anne contest at one p.m. All participants had to provide their own costume, and in Rosy's category (eleven and up), they would have to display some kind of talent, as well as demonstrate a "visible portrayal of personality."

Helen looked at Rosy. "It says you'll be required to answer questions about *Anne of Green Gables*, and you'll have to present a piece from the book or sing a song."

Rosy wasn't the least bit worried about her personality or her flair for the dramatic. But she looked about as much like Anne as Mr. Wing looked like Elvis. (Although that didn't stop him from donning sideburns and bell-bottom pants and singing "Blue Suede Shoes" at the holiday dinner put on by the local homeless shelter. Everyone applauded and cheered as if it was the King himself. Mr. Wing didn't realize that it was really the moo goo guy pan he donated to the dinner that they were cheering for.)

Rosy'd often thought about going to Westfield Village because the Anne movie had been filmed there. Although she hadn't seen the movie, she would have loved to sit on the bench in front of the Bright River train station. A fabricated Prince Edward Island would be better than none at all. But Rosy had no way to get to Rockton.

"It's not very far down Highway 8, dear," said Helen, trying to be helpful. But it might as well have been on the moon. If the bus didn't go there, neither did Rosy. Helen wouldn't give up. "Doesn't your oldest brother drive?"

"He got his license when he started working for Mr. Wing." (Ben was determined to save money, but by Rosy's calculations he'd have to deliver Chinese food until he was forty-eight to pay for his first year of medical school.)

"Anyway, Helen, we don't have a car." Rosy handed her back the flyer. "Other than Mr. Spinelli, none of my neighbors drive. And he only takes his car as far as the grocery store. Jay and Sebastian have a scooter – that's it." Helen said she wished she could take Rosy, but she had to work that afternoon.

At any rate, what did it matter? As much as she'd love to win those books, Rosy didn't look a bit like Anne of Green Gables.

But she knew everything about her. Everything.

And how else could she get that boxed set? Every Christmas she hoped for something from Operation Santa Claus. But Robin was the kind of mother who made sure her kids contributed to the charity, instead of benefiting from it.

In July, Rosy and her brothers helped with the charity's big garage sale on the beach strip. Then in December, they distributed gifts to kids and seniors who would otherwise go without. Christmas was spent understanding the meaning of Christmas. (It meant you didn't ask for anything.)

Rosy didn't buy into the whole "better to give than receive" thing the way her mother did. She wished she could be like that. Sometimes she worried she was selfish like her father.

But she knew her mother couldn't afford to spend money on books that were right there on the shelves of the library, so she never asked. She'd have to put up with the used and abused copies, that's all.

Rosy got to thinking that maybe all the time she was forced to spend in the library might pay off after all. By reading the stories again and again, she had come to memorize entire sections. Maybe the judges *would* buy the idea of a Native Anne with long dark braids. (No, that would never work.) Maybe Ben could borrow Mr. Spinelli's Pontiac.

One door was off and it had duct tape on the windshield, but at least it went. The problem would be persuading him to let it out of his sight for a couple hours.

And what would she do for a costume? She'd likely wind up at the thrift shop, fishing through stuff to throw something together; but the girls who could afford to have a costume made for them would look much more authentic. That is, if they knew what they were doing. If they went with the usual flowered blouse, green pinafore, and white stockings instead of the ugly, yellowish-gray wincey Anne was wearing when Matthew brought her home, they didn't stand a chance. Maybe there'd be an ugly, yellowish-gray dress at the thrift store. Everything else she got there was ugly.

Maybe she *could* win this thing. There wasn't a single question she couldn't answer. Maybe she should enter. Maybe she should try.

Chapter 3

Rosy used her pass and took the bus downtown. It was the Saturday after Helen had told her about the contest, and Helen had convinced her to go to an information session at the library's main branch. They were going to explain the contest and give sample questions. Rosy was sure she didn't need any help, but decided to check out her competition.

There were beautiful things in the store windows at Jackson Square. She wished she could buy clothes like that. She wished her mother could have clothes like that. She wished her stuff wasn't always secondhand. She wished she didn't have to worry that someone would recognize what she was wearing. She wished her mother had more than one nice dress. (Turquoise with navy blue flowers and made of a sort of floaty material. Robin looked like a movie star in it.)

It was eleven-thirty, so Rosy headed to the library entrance. The children's department was on the ground level, but she wanted to walk across the top of the square first so she could look up at all the tall, important-looking buildings. People came and people went, doors opened and doors shut, but no one said much. For Rosy, it was the buildings that did all the talking. They told her to reach for the sky.

When she got inside the library, there were fifteen or so girls sitting in a circle on the floor, and the speaker was about to begin. Rosy took a place in the back.

Two girls pointed at her and whispered something to each other. She hoped – she *prayed* – she wasn't wearing one of their old tops or their shorts or their shoes. (She worried most about the tops. People remember their tops.)

Rosy was the only one there with black hair. Maybe that was why they were whispering. She hoped that was why. Maybe she would go with the Native Anne theme after all.

"Okay girls, I want your attention now." The librarian held both arms in the air until everyone stopped talking. "My name is Mrs. Pratt, and I want to thank you all for coming out to this information session brought to you by the Hamilton Public Library and the Westfield Heritage

Village." Rosy's mind had already started to wander. "Today we will be going over the rules for the contest thoroughly, and I will answer any of your questions to the best of my ability. Light refreshments will be served at noon. Please do not handle any books while drinking or eating."

Just as Mrs. Pratt began giving details of the contest, another girl walked in. Rather than letting her take a seat quietly, the woman made a point of stopping midway through a sentence, drawing as much attention as possible to the fact that the girl was late. The girl stumbled over Rosy's foot, then fell down next to her. (Rosy hadn't meant to trip her, but she decided she might try it later – on the two girls who were pointing.)

"I…I'm sorry." The latecomer's apology was not acknowledged; Mrs. Pratt ignored her and picked up the other half of her sentence exactly where she left off.

"…in the age eleven and over category will be expected to have a thorough knowledge of Miss Montgomery's book." While she rambled on, Rosy glanced at the girl beside her. Without a shadow of a doubt, she looked exactly like Anne: pale, skinny, with orangey-red hair and green eyes that were way too big for her face. And pronounced front teeth.

The Anne clone stared into her notebook and wrote down every word Mrs. Pratt said. She smelled like cherry Life Savers. Rosy didn't write anything down. There was nothing she didn't know about Anne already, and the only ideas about costumes involved purchasing things (which she couldn't do). Then it was time for questions.

"I have a question, Mrs. Pratt."

"What is your query?" asked the woman, wiping her forehead with a tissue.

"What do they mean by a 'visible portrayal of personality'?" asked Rosy, with her hands in her back pockets.

"This refers to the fact the judges will be making their choice based not only on a physical resemblance to Miss Montgomery's heroine, but also to the degree each contestant can portray the true character of this young girl."

Good, thought Rosy. *That means I have a chance.*

No one else had a question, so the meeting ended early. Mrs. Pratt handed out sheets with examples of what to expect at the contest, along with paper cups and plates. The light refreshments were pink water, which was probably lemonade, and cheese-spread sandwiches. But it was free. Rosy decided to talk to the Anne clone.

"Hi. My name is Rosy Taylor and I am half Mohawk. My birthday is August twenty-second, so I am a Leo. I will be twelve. Who are you?"

"How do you do? I am Lydia Parker and I don't know what a Leo is. Pleased to meet you." She held out a limp white hand, which felt cold and bony when Rosy shook it.

"Leo is a zodiac sign. Leo people are self-confident and exuberant and they are born actors. It is the most dynamic sign of the zodiac." Rosy lifted an eyebrow. "You don't ever want to get on the bad side of a Leo."

"Maybe I'm a Leo too," said Lydia. "Although I don't think I'm dynamic. I'll be twelve on August twenty-fourth."

"Oh, *please*," replied Rosy, gulping back more pink water, "you're not a Leo, you are a Virgo. But don't let anyone call you dull. It is not so much that you are boring – you are actually practical and careful."

"No one has ever called me dull," said Lydia. There was a smear of cheese spread on her front tooth. "Until now."

Rosy continued talking. "I think Anne must have been an Aries. We know from the book she was born in March, and there is no way she could be a Pisces. No, her fiery nature means she is definitely an Aries. Like my mother." Rosy gazed out the window of the library. "And since I am a Leo, which is also a fire sign, Anne and I have similar personalities."

Lydia looked dejected and pathetic, too, with that cheese on her tooth. "I guess I haven't much hope, being a Virgo."

"Well, Lydia," admitted Rosy, "you do bear a striking resemblance to the orphan. You're skinny and pale, you have carrot-red hair, and your eyes are too big. If I was the judge of this contest, and the contest was based solely on appearance, you would win." She stood up, took a handful of sandwiches from the table and stuck them into her bag. "For the road," she said when Mrs. Pratt gave her a dirty look.

She plunked herself back down beside Lydia and continued. "Of course, I still plan on winning this thing, so don't get any big ideas about taking home the prize."

Lydia opened up a roll of cherry Life Savers and offered one to Rosy. She took two.

"What is that?" Lydia wondered what was sticking out of Rosy's pocket.

"You mean you've never seen an inhaler before? Where do you go to school...on Mars?" At Rosy's school, so many kids suffered from asthma, classes consisted of reading, writing, and the proper use of fast-acting bronchodilators.

"Oh, gosh, I'm sorry. I didn't realize what it was." Lydia's face turned patchy and red, and her freckles got bigger.

"Forget about it."

Rosy asked for another Life Saver, and Lydia told her to keep the roll. *Typical Virgo,* thought Rosy. *Always helpful. Always trying to please.* That gave her an idea. Lydia became Plan B.

"Do you have a car in your family?" she asked the Anne clone, figuring it might be a way for her to get to Rockton if all else failed. Lydia said she did, so Rosy invited Plan B to come for lunch the next day at her place.

Chapter 4

"Here she comes!" yelled John, who'd been watching out the front window while Rosy set the lunch table with paper serviettes. "She looks like she came out from under a rock."

Lydia tripped over the mat at the door. When Rosy introduced her to her brothers, she stood stock still like a robot and peered over the tops of their heads. Rosy figured she was pretending they were in their underwear, like they tell you to do when you're nervous on stage.

"You'll never guess what Mom made for lunch – potato soup," declared Rosy. "This is destiny. This means the stars are behind me – uh, us." She handed Lydia a raw potato.

"What does soup have to do with the stars?" asked Lydia politely, putting the potato into her canvas bag.

"These are Prince Edward Island spuds! They were grown in Summerside. Isn't that a great name – Summerside?" She grabbed another potato from the sack and rubbed it. "See this? It's genuine dirt from the island. It works like pixie dust."

"You won't believe what she does whenever she gets a P.E.I. potato, Lydia," said Patrick, taking his place at the table. "She sleeps with it under her pillow. She won't throw it out until it turns black!" The two younger boys cackled and snorted. Rosy thought they were idiots. Lydia thought they were wonderful.

Rosy's mom put a big plate of rolls on the table and told Lydia she could sit beside Rosy.

"If you sleep on it," Rosy explained, "you will dream you are Anne, and you're driving along the shore road with Matthew in the carriage, or you're watching the birches in the hollow wave good morning, or you're telling Mrs. Lynde you *hate* her – *hate* her – **HATE** her, or you're floating down the stream as the Lily Maid, or you're—"

"All that from one potato?" asked Ben, reaching for the rolls. "So where do you go to school, Lydia?" The girl, startled when he spoke to her, spilled a whole spoonful of soup down the front of her blouse. It sat in a big lump at first, then slowly dribbled down her buttons. Rosy tried to get it off with a serviette, then finally grabbed a dishcloth and mopped it up.

"Sorry about the buns," said Rosy, noticing Lydia hadn't touched hers. "Mom would have heated them up, but the element in the oven isn't working."

"They're fine," said Lydia.

Ben spoke to her again. "Do you have any brothers or sisters?"

"No," replied Lydia, looking to the left of his head. "I'm an only child." Rosy wished she'd stop doing that robot thing. She sounded like one of those dolls that talk when you push a button in its back.

Rosy's mother sensed the girl's tension. "So you two don't have much time before the big day. Rosy's been scouting around everywhere for things to make a costume with, but she hasn't had any luck."

"Yeah," admitted Rosy. "I've been through every dress at the Salvation Army, and the only one that even came close was a gray jumper. But it had grape juice stains on it." Rosy choked on a big chunk of roll. "So is your mother going to make a costume for you, Lydia?"

"My mother lives in London, England. She and her new husband have twins."

"So you're not an only child!" quipped John.

"No, I guess I'm not."

"So, where do you go to school?" Ben persisted with the question, and since everyone was waiting for an answer, Lydia knew she couldn't avoid it any longer. She dropped her spoon on the floor; Rosy picked it up and got her another one. *What a klutz,* she thought.

"Hillfield-Strathallan."

"So you're a rich kid, then?" Patrick didn't beat around the bush. Rosy kicked him under the table. "Well, she must be rich to go to private school!"

"Hey, what kind of car does your father drive? A Mercedes or a Lamborghini?" John's passion in life was automobiles – even Mr. Spinelli's old Pontiac. Lydia stopped talking altogether.

The next fifteen minutes felt like ten days. Rosy wished she'd never met this girl.

She decided to get through the afternoon, then never see Lydia again. Anyway, she was sure Lydia was disgusted with her home. She must have thought the paper serviettes were a joke. Girls like her have cloth napkins that some maid washes and irons. Girls like her don't live in a dump. Why did she ever give her that stupid potato? She wished she could get it back. Maybe if Lydia went to use the bathroom, Rosy would grab the potato from her bag and hurl it out the window. If she was lucky, it would ping Patrick in the head.

"I think your mother is lovely. She looks like one of the stars in those classic old movies." She didn't sound like a talking doll once she got away from the boys, up in Rosy's room.

Rosy acted casual, but she was proud as a peacock that Lydia had noticed her mother was pretty. Still, she thought Lydia was clueless. All Lydia really wanted to do was chat about Rosy's brothers. She wanted to know everything about them. She didn't say much about her own life, except that she had a new housekeeper, Mrs. Allison, who she hoped would last longer than the others.

Rosy couldn't squeeze any fun out of Lydia whatsoever; she was worse than the end of a ketchup bottle. Rosy swore off Virgos for life. She had hoped Lydia would have turned out to be a good friend, a kindred spirit like Diana was to Anne. But no rich kid could ever be a kindred spirit. No way.

And if there was any doubt about Lydia's wealth, it soon vaporized when a taxi came to pick her up. (She'd arrived in one, too, but Rosy's brother hadn't noticed.)

No one in the north end ever took a taxi unless they were sick and ready to die, or in labor.

The neighbors stood in a row on the sidewalk to see who was dying. As the taxi pulled away, Lydia smiled, poked her hand out the rear window, and waved to the crowd.

Mr. Spinelli, out washing the remains of his Pontiac, waved back and yelled, "*Arrivederci!* Good-bye! Have a good day!" then returned to his singing. Actually, he never stopped singing. It helped drown out his wife, who never stopped hollering at him. Mr. Spinelli had a decent voice but would stay with one song for weeks, which meant that during the summer months, when folks had their windows open, the melody would go through their heads over and over again.

Jay and Sebastian were sitting on the stairs in front of their half of the house.

"Who's your new friend?" asked Jay, humming and tapping his feet to Mr. Spinelli's tune.

"She's not my friend. Not really." Rosy sat down on the step and rested her chin in her hand. "She's going to be in the contest next month."

The two men exchanged glances.

"You'd better get yourself a good costume, Rosy." Sebastian put his arm around her back. "That girl is the spitting image of Anne of Green Gables."

Chapter 5

"I never thought you were a snob, Rosy. Are you too special to spend a day at Lydia's?" Robin was washing dinner plates at the sink, and Rosy was drying. "The poor girl has phoned here every day this week, and you treat her like...like..."

"Like a rich kid, Mom? Well, she is a rich kid and rich kids should hang around other rich kids; they can compare wish lists and play badminton and eat mint sherbet."

"Mint sherbet, Rosy?"

"Rich kids smell like mint. And dark chocolate. And leather."

"Well, I thought you were tougher than that. I thought you could deal, but I guess you're a bit of a coward after all." Robin handed Rosy the last plate and sat down at the kitchen table. "Listen Rosy, when Lydia calls the next time, your brothers and I are not going to make up excuses for you."

"You won't have to make them up. I am providing you with a list of seventeen good reasons why I can't come to the phone." She handed the list to her mother, who started to laugh when she read down the page.

"Oh, come on Rosy. The army? I'm pretty sure the army won't take eleven-year-olds."

In her heart of hearts, Rosy knew her mother had hit the nail on the head when she said she was tough enough to handle any situation. She was no coward.

So what if Lydia was filthy rich and lived in a great big mansion? She was, nevertheless, a Virgo, and naive about the real world. Besides, Rosy hadn't yet asked Mr. Spinelli if they could borrow his Pontiac, so there remained the issue of the ride to Rockton. Lydia was still Plan B.

"Okay, you win. I'll do it. I'll persevere through another deadly boring day with Lydia to prove to you I don't care how rich she is."

"And yourself, Rosy. You'll prove it to yourself."

The next afternoon, Rosy took the bus up the mountain. Lydia's directions were useless at best, but no wonder. All she'd ever learned to do was hop in a cab and say, "Home please," and off she went.

Rosy didn't want to wear anything that might be recognized on Lydia's street, so she borrowed one of John's T-shirts that had a union logo on the front and the slogan "Keep Labor Working" on the back. She figured nobody had a T-shirt like that in Lydia's neighborhood.

She also made sure her visit would take place after lunch and before dinner. She did not want to eat anything at a table with rich people, because if they set out more than one fork, she wouldn't know which one to use.

Her mother told her to watch how the others chose their cutlery, but being a vegetarian, eating at other people's places was always a problem for Rosy. She hated the perennial argument that animals were put on the planet for us to eat, so everyone should.

Her counterargument – that maybe everyone should take up smoking then, since tobacco was put on the planet too – usually landed on deaf ears.

Sometimes, people would try sarcasm. "Well, you're willing to kill a cabbage aren't you?" That was where Jay and Sebastian's "nothing that blinks" always came in handy.

It was one-thirty when the bus driver let Rosy off at the end of a winding boulevard that ran along the edge of the mountain. She walked quite a few blocks, shaded by a canopy of tall, leafy trees, the kind that only grew at the top of the Hamilton escarpment, where the air was cleaner. Finally, she found Lydia's place.

It was indeed a mansion. A great big huge prodigious mansion. Any faint glimmer of hope that Lydia was just well-to-do, and not disgustingly rich, evaporated faster than the mist from her massive water fountain in the hot August sun. There was even a courtyard in the middle of the lawn, which in Rosy's neighborhood would have made a dandy park for at least a hundred people and their pets.

She opened up the wrought-iron gate, shut it behind her, then ventured toward the house. In her old shorts and brother's T-shirt, she didn't look like a visitor. She looked like she was in the wrong neighborhood.

A man appeared from inside a circle of cedar hedges wielding a spade. He turned out to be the gardener who, in a gentle voice, said, "Hi there. I'm Dex." He was stunningly handsome, and Rosy thought he'd be a perfect match for her mom – if only she hadn't sworn off men for life. Rosy liked the way he smelled: of fresh earth and leaves. "You must be here to see Lydia," he said.

"Yes, sir." Rosy had never met a real gardener before. In the north end, the closest thing to a gardener was the man from the Hamilton Parks Department, and all he did was plant petunias once a year and pick up garbage the rest of the time.

The front door opened, and an exceptionally tall, stern-looking woman, with a shock of gray hair and wearing a white apron, came out and picked up the newspaper. Her forehead took up more than half her face. The only other person Rosy knew with a forehead like that was the undertaker on Barton Street, who carried a measuring tape in his pocket to scare the kids with.

The woman noticed Rosy (who was beginning to wonder if she'd better get out while she still could) and beckoned her toward the house – in a sort of grim way – using her long, pointed index finger.

Rosy found herself walking with a stiff gait, like a bride or somebody in a parade. The housekeeper closed the door behind her and called for Lydia.

While she was waiting for Lydia to come down the spiral staircase (which took three minutes), Rosy looked around the hall. Everything was polished wood and brass. You could see your own reflection no matter where you turned, like in the house of mirrors at the carnival. The chair at the front door was ornately carved, and the paintings on the walls were a lot different from the prints Rosy's mother had bought in garage sales. Definitely no clowns or scenes of Niagara Falls for these folks.

"Hi, Rosy!" called Lydia from halfway up the staircase. "Come on up."

Once again, Rosy found herself walking weirdly. She couldn't get her legs to move normally. It was a relief to get to the top. She hung over the balcony and felt like bursting into song – until she noticed the housekeeper staring at her from behind the kitchen door.

Lydia's bedroom was high up in a tower room that soared over Hamilton. Rosy looked toward the north end of the city, trying to locate her house; she could see nothing but a cloud of murky gray haze with the occasional building sticking out, gasping for air.

The room was pink – a ghastly sort of bubblegum pink – but pink nonetheless. Pink canopy bed, pink telephone, pink satin bedspread, pink broadloom, pink ruffled curtains, pink wallpaper consisting of pink stripes with pink rosettes.

But Rosy wasn't jealous – not really. None of it bothered her, although she still regretted giving a potato to a rich girl. No, none of it bothered Rosy at all. Not a bit. Then, in the middle of hundreds and hundreds of dollars worth of dolls, videos, DVDs, and books, she spotted several copies of *Anne of Green Gables*; hard cover, soft cover, the illustrated version, the annotated version. And it bothered her. It *really* bothered her.

"Okay Lydia, I'm outta' here." Rosy took off.

Chapter 6

Lydia grabbed Rosy's T-shirt, sprung her back like she was a yo-yo, then pulled her into the room. "What's wrong, Rosy? You just arrived. Can't you stay a while longer?" Lydia threw open the dresser-drawer beside her, pulled out a roll of Life Savers, stuck one in her mouth, and handed the rest to Rosy, who was thinking Lydia must have a pretty mean left hook.

"You know, you're getting seriously addicted to these things." Rosy confiscated four unopened rolls from Lydia's drawer. "Okay, so you've got to begin by switching to orange, then yellow, then green, and gradually wean yourself off them altogether. You Virgos are prone to these kinds of problems." She went to leave again, then turned around and faced Lydia.

"I don't get it," she snapped. "Why are you entering this contest if you've already got so many *Anne* books? Is it for the trophy?"

Lydia sat down on the edge of her bed. "I'd like to have the boxed set, but that's not my reason for entering."

"Okay, I'm listening. You've got sixty seconds." Rosy leaned against the wall and crossed her arms in front, as if to say, "but I don't really care."

"The potato worked, you know," said Lydia, reaching under her pillow. She pulled out the wrinkly spud. "I had a dream about Anne. I had a dream that I won the contest, and my father came and he saw me win and he was so proud of me." Lydia got up and walked over to the window that overlooked the backyard. "And *she* wasn't there!" She pointed out the window. Things were getting interesting.

Rosy took a look, examining the situation. Beside the mammoth kidney-shaped swimming pool, sunning herself in a yellow one-piece bathing suit, was a tanned, athletic-looking blond woman.

"I have one question," said Rosy. "Why on earth are you so pale when you've got a swimming pool like that? You should be in it every day – not up in this tower!"

"I can't go out in the sun and I can't swim." Lydia caught her foot on the rug and tripped over a stuffed bear. "I get the pink eye."

"Well you've certainly got an eye for pink!" Rosy cackled, but Lydia was too upset to laugh at anything.

"Okay, okay," said Rosy, "so tell me about the lady by the pool." Just as she asked the question, she saw the housekeeper hand the woman a glass of something white. "What's that milky stuff?"

"It's some kind of special Chinese energy drink." Lydia made a face. "Tastes awful."

"And what's with your housekeeper? She looks like she's been drinking it too."

"Mrs. Harmon?"

"Harmon?" asked Rosy. "I thought you said your house-keeper was Mrs. Allison?"

"She was…until yesterday," replied Lydia, opening up a new roll of Life Savers, this time from a box in her closet. "But right now, the only thing that matters is this contest because it's my one chance to get an hour or two with my dad without Tiffany hanging on his arm."

"He sounds like a busy man," said Rosy. "Is he an astronaut or something?"

"Oh, Rosy. You're mean. How can you be so mean, with everything you've got?" Lydia was serious.

"Everything *I've* got? Let me see…I've got a bed, some clothes that once sat in somebody else's dirty laundry hamper, a discarded copy of *Anne of Green Gables* that looks like it fell in a mud puddle, a bedspread Mom got on sale because there was an ugly black mark on what was once a frill, shoes I can only hope didn't belong to someone with athlete's foot, two sticks of gum, a bath towel I found that says "Stolen from the Flamingo Motel," a radio that gets only one station, a harmonica I won at the Dundas summer festival, and the food in my stomach. Oh, and four and a half rolls of cherry Life Savers. That's everything I got." Rosy pointed to Lydia's shelves of stuff. "Now, shall we do your inventory?"

"I wasn't talking about *things*, I meant you have so much going for you. Your mother...your brothers." Lydia looked out the window again. "What is your father like?"

Rosy didn't want to talk about James Taylor, Taylor James, Jimmy Bing, or Bing Taylor. So she came up with someone else. "My father is an Indian chief, and you're not likely to see him too often. He has important land claims to make, stuff like that."

"I thought you said you were only half Mohawk." Rosy had forgotten that Virgos have good memories and that to be a good liar, you have to recall what you said and when.

"Yes, I am half Mohawk, and my father is American. So he is, ah...he is...in Nevada. He's...Shawnee."

"But the Shawnees are in Oklahoma. Nevada is home to the Navajos." Lydia might not be street-wise, but she sure knew her tribes. The only thing to do was change the subject completely.

"So what about *your* father, Lydia?" asked Rosy. "If he's not an astronaut, then what does he do? Let me guess. He owns the Hamilton Tiger-cats football team."

"He's a cardiologist and heart surgeon at the Hamilton General and teaches at McMaster University. He's never home. I've spent more time with the mailman than I have with my own dad." Rosy went to laugh, but realized Lydia didn't mean it as a joke. "And any time he does have goes to *her*." She pointed toward the pool again, then buried her head in her hands.

"Who is she, anyway?"

"She's Tiffany Lee," answered a red-faced, teary-eyed Lydia. "She does the TV sportscast on the six o'clock news and she's horrible. She pretends to like me, but I can tell she wishes I was nowhere around." Lydia paused for a minute. "She's a sports nut. Swims all summer and plays hockey all winter." She paused again. "She'd like me better if I was good at sports."

"Don't you like sports?" wondered Rosy.

"I hate sports. I hate all sports."

"Even badminton?" She wanted to test her rich-kids theory.

"Even badminton."

Rosy was beginning to think she must have been wrong about rich kids. "How do you feel about mint sherbet?"

Lydia was about to respond when the bedroom door swung open and Tiffany strolled in. She smelled like chlorine with a twist of strong cologne. "Hi, girls. I came to meet your new friend, Lydia. I bet you two were talking about boys, weren't you?" She threw herself down on the bed, then rolled over, leaving a wet mark where her backside had been.

"Actually," replied Rosy, "we were planning our robbery – going over the floor plan of the National Bank. You know, to map out all the entrances and exits." Rosy was trying to be funny, but Tiffany didn't respond. She stared at Rosy, then continued.

"So does your friend have a name, Lydia?"

Rosy tried again. "The Brains."

Tiffany didn't laugh that time either.

She turned to Rosy. "What are you, a comedian or something?"

Rosy popped another red Life Saver in her mouth. (Having met Dr. Parker's girlfriend, she had gained a new understanding of the root of Lydia's addiction to the candies.) Rosy was having trouble breathing, so she leaned on the wall again.

"She's not a comedian," asserted Lydia. "She's just funny,

that's all." Lydia was proud of her new friend. "Her name is Rosy and she's a Leo. And she's half Native, too."

Rosy asked Lydia for directions to the washroom (which turned out to be only slightly clearer than the ones she'd given to her house).

When Rosy returned, Tiffany was giving advice to Lydia.

"Well, I hope you don't ask her to stay the night. And whatever you do, don't let her use your hairbrush and don't use hers. She could have head lice and they're contagious. Before you know it, you'll be scratching and itching. And you know, tuberculosis is no longer a thing of the past. That could be why she's having trouble breathing."

"Rosy doesn't have tuberculosis, she has asthma."

"Well, I don't think she's the kind of girl your father—"

The normally impenetrable Rosy felt like she had been stung by a thousand bees. She felt dirty. She felt ashamed. Finally, she felt nothing at all.

Nothing at all.

Then she did what she always does; she dealt.

"Let me tell you right now that other than one bad case of poison ivy at the Salvation Army summer day camp, when we hiked through the Red Hill Creek Valley, neither my brothers nor myself have ever itched. My mother – who is way better looking than you, by the way—"

"She is," declared Lydia.

"Anyway," continued Rosy, still in a rage, "head lice doesn't just favor the north end, you know." And Rosy wasn't finished. "Of course, *you* don't have to worry about lice, because nothing could ever survive in that much bleach."

"She's right!" yelled Lydia.

"I've never known you to be so nasty, Lydia." Tiffany glared at Rosy. "I guess it's the company you're keeping these days."

"Well," replied Lydia, "Rosy was only defending herself. It wasn't very nice of you to imply that she had TB."

"TB?" A man's voice came from outside the bedroom door. It was Dr. Parker, Lydia's father. "What's this about TB?"

Chapter 7

Lydia ran to her father and tried to give him a hug, but Tiffany had gotten there first. Lydia tried again, but he turned the other direction and removed his jacket instead. Rosy could see he wasn't the responsive type, so she walked over and introduced herself.

"Hello. My name is Rosy Taylor and my birthday is on Thursday. I am half Mohawk. I am not a comedian, like Tiffany assumed. I am a Leo, which means I have a flair for the dramatic, and I am pleased to meet you." She stuck out her hand. "Oh, and by the way, despite what you might have overheard, I do not have head lice, nor do I have tuberculosis, but I do suffer from asthma. Maybe you could explain the causes of this condition to Tiffany and assure her that

I will not pass it on to Lydia. She has no more chance of catching asthma from me than I do of becoming a Virgo from spending time with her."

Dr. Parker shook Rosy's hand. "Well, that's all very interesting," he said flatly. Then he looked at his watch. "What's this about TB?"

Before Lydia or Rosy could respond, the phone rang.

"You see what I mean?" said Lydia, and Rosy understood why she needed a contest to capture her father's attention. Still, she didn't feel much like sticking around.

"Well, Lydia, I think I'll be going now."

"But it's only two-thirty! Please stay." Lydia begged her not to leave, but Rosy wanted to go home and check for lice in the mirror.

"Lydia," called her father. "It's your mother. She wants to know what you want for your birthday."

The girl flew to the phone and grabbed it out of her father's hand.

"Mom!"

Rosy could hear the mumble of Lydia's mother's voice through the receiver. It sounded like she had a British accent.

"Mom, can you come home for my…" More mumbling, then Lydia replied, "Well, I don't really play with dolls anymore. I'd love it if you could be here…" She hesitated, then continued, "...but I guess you're busy with the twins."

Lydia's mother talked for a minute or so.

"Mom, do you remember the night when we stayed up until midnight to watch that old movie you love, *Gone with the Wind*? Maybe we could rent a copy sometime and..."

Her mother interrupted with another suggestion.

"I have quite a few sweaters, but that sounds nice," muttered Lydia. Another pause. "Bye, Mom." She went to put down the phone, then had a second thought. "Mom... Mom?" She tried to catch her, but her mother had already hung up.

Lydia faced Rosy, the phone still in her hand. "I wanted to tell her about the contest."

Rosy left quietly, without saying much. In some ways it was a relief to leave the mountain and return to the north end, even though the smog was bothering her more than usual. She got off at Sanford Avenue and cut through the back alley to her place. Her mother was sitting on the steps with Jay and Sebastian, who had just finished styling hair for fifteen bridesmaids and had taken the rest of the afternoon off to recover.

"What are you doing back so soon?" Her mother seemed worried. "Okay, so what did you do?"

Rosy avoided the question by asking another one.

"Do I have lice?" she asked Jay and Sebastian, figuring they of all people would know. "Is there anything crawling around on my head?" She parted her hair with both hands and bent forward for them to take a look.

"Yeah," said Jay, "there is something in there." He started to pick away at her scalp.

"Oh no, she was right!" Rosy was horrified.

"Wait a minute…it's just a…it's some kind of pink fluff or something." Jay pulled out the pink fiber and handed it to Sebastian.

"Definitely not lice," he said, smiling at Rosy.

"Okay, everyone," declared Robin, "the fun is over. So what the heck is all this about lice? And you still haven't explained why you only stayed thirty seconds at Lydia's."

"Who said you have head lice?" Sebastian looked puzzled.

"This woman named Tiffany Lee. She's Lydia's father's girlfriend."

"You don't mean Tiffany Lee the sportscaster?" asked Jay.

"Yeah, that's her." Rosy sat down. "Do you know her?"

"I sure do. I've done her hair many times. Frankly, I've found her to be awfully bossy." Jay turned to Sebastian. "She's quite an athlete, though…played hockey in a league of some sort. And somebody told me she almost made the

Olympic swimming team. I don't know if that's true, but her real color is brown. I am *sure* of that."

"Rosy," interrupted Robin, "Were you rude to this woman?"

"Well, she deserved it, Mom. She told Lydia she shouldn't be around me because I might give her lice. So I told her that she's one person who'd never have to worry about it, being as she had so much bleach on her head."

"Bravo!" yelled Jay.

Rosy looked at her mother. "I was actually sticking up for Lydia, too. Tiffany doesn't want her around and Lydia can sense it."

"*Now* I know who she is!" exclaimed Sebastian. "Tall. Always drinking that Chinese energy stuff. Her color is Moonlight in Morocco, right?"

"That's her!" said Jay.

"I didn't realize she was a local celebrity." Jay and Sebastian didn't bother with television.

"Lydia says Tiffany doesn't like her because she hates sports," said Rosy.

"Okay, young lady." Robin wasn't amused by any of it. "Get right back on the next bus and apologize to this woman and I mean it. I don't care what she said to you, you can't talk like that to Lydia's…whatever she is."

"I also told her you were way prettier than her."

"Oh my goodness! Get going, Rosy!" Robin wouldn't take no for an answer.

"But she told Lydia I might have tuberculosis!"

"Well, that is ridiculous. Are you okay now?"

"I guess. But will you come with me?" If she had to go back to Lydia's tower, she at least wanted Tiffany (not to mention the gardener) to see her naturally beautiful mother.

"Okay, okay. I'll ride with you on the bus. That way I'll be sure you set things right."

"Will you wear that turquoise dress with the blue flowers?" Rosy didn't want her to wear her work uniform.

"No, I will not. Now let's get going, or I'll be late for work."

"You know," said Jay, "I don't want to interfere, but Tiffany is kind of nasty. She doesn't treat people at the salon very well, either." He felt sorry for Rosy, having to apologize to the disagreeable woman. "She had no right to say those things to our Rosy."

"I don't care if she's the devil herself, Rosy cannot be encouraged to be rude." Robin grabbed her purse and called in the door to let the boys know she was leaving.

"Well, we'll see you two later. *Bonne Chance!*" Jay called to Robin and Rosy as they headed down the alley, then turned to his friend. "They're going to need it."

Sebastian thought for a minute before he spoke. "Moonlight in Morocco is a dreadful shade."

"I know," said Jay. "Why do you think I picked it out for her?"

Chapter 8

During the bus ride up the mountain, Rosy thought about Anne and her famous fight with Mrs. Rachel Lynde. How she told Marilla she'd rather be locked up in a dark, damp dungeon inhabited by snakes than have to apologize. How she'd rather starve than give in to the nasty woman. Rosy felt the same, so she was trying a few scenarios in her head.

Her mother interrupted her thoughts. "You know, Rosy, you've got less than two weeks to put a costume together. Have you asked Jay and Sebastian for help? They said they could find you some red hair." Robin looked out the window of the bus as it climbed the mountain access. She couldn't stand heights, and was seated on the cliff side, so she turned her back to the window.

Rosy figured she'd talk to the hairdressers when she got home, and maybe head over to the library for more practice questions from Helen. There was no way she could lose as far as knowledge of the books went, but the costume was another story. She'd rifled through bargain bins at the thrift shop the day before, but nothing was right. There was one dress that might have done, but it was too small.

"Well," said Rosy, hating to admit it, "this is our stop."

When they got to Lydia's, and through the gates, she noticed her mom's walk was weird too. Rosy tried to stall for time so the handsome gardener would have a chance to meet Robin, but he wasn't around. Lydia's father's red Porsche was in the driveway, which meant he was still home.

Rosy rang the bell (which wasn't a north end buzz. It was a rich person's ding ding ding-ling-ling, ding ding ding dong). Mrs. Harmon answered the door with a look on her face that made Rosy feel like she and her mother were campaigning to buy a new trombone for the Salvation Army band.

"Can I help you?" she asked in a rigid voice, as if she'd never seen Rosy in her life, let alone an hour before.

"It's me again."

"Wait here," she cautioned, and they stood outside until Dr. Parker asked them in.

"Let me call Lydia." He yelled loudly enough that his voice could be heard upstairs, but kept looking back at Robin. "LY-di-a. LY-di-a. Your friend is here again." Then he took them into the living room, and they sat down on a sofa so big and so soft that it almost put Rosy to sleep.

"I'm Rosy's mother," Robin began, "and we're here so that Rosy can apologize in person to your friend for being impolite. I don't raise my children to speak out of turn, and I don't know what prompted her to act in that way. I'm sorry…Doctor…uh…" Robin realized she didn't know Lydia's last name.

"Dr. Parker," replied Rosy.

"From what Tiffany tells me, it was a misunderstanding, that's all," he maintained.

We understood each other perfectly, said Rosy to herself.

"Thank you, but my daughter obviously needs a lesson in manners. And she will apologize." Robin was resolute.

Just as Robin was beginning to wonder if anyone would ever show up, Tiffany rushed into the room and threw herself down beside the doctor. At first, she didn't pay much attention to the visitors, taking time only to give Rosy a dirty look. Then she saw Robin.

Rosy stood up, put her hands behind her back, took as deep a breath as she could, and proceeded with the apology. She could smell cherry Life Savers coming from behind the hall door and furniture wax from the other end of the room, so she knew both Lydia and Mrs. Harmon were listening.

"Without any further ado," Rosy began, "I truly want to express my heartfelt apologies for saying the terrible things I said to you. I should not have mentioned your bleached-blond hair. It was wrong of me, even if you did say I had head lice and tuberculosis."

"You said *what*?" Dr. Parker looked directly at Tiffany. (Now she was in trouble.) "I can't believe you would say something like that."

Lydia came out from behind the door. Mrs. Harmon did not emerge, but Rosy knew she was still looming.

"She sure did." Lydia stumbled over the leg of the coffee table. "Dad…"

Tiffany tried to break up the conversation by reminding Dr. Parker that there were salads waiting for them by the pool and the lettuce was wilting.

"Can you stay for a cup of coffee, Mrs. Taylor?" asked Lydia's father.

"No, thank you," replied Robin politely. "I have to be getting to work." She stood up and reached for her purse, signaling Rosy that it was time to go.

"Oh, Rosy, can't you stay? Please?" Lydia begged her for the second time that day.

"No, I've got to talk to these guys to see if they found me a wig, and I've got to see Helen at the library." She walked with her mother to the front door. "She's been asking me questions so I'll be ready for the judges. I want to be sure that I know every little detail. You've got to find someone to do that for you. Someone like...like..." Rosy knew Tiffany wasn't the type to help, and her father had fewer spare minutes in a day than it took to make a cup of instant coffee. "Someone like Mrs. Harmon," she said, squinting to see through the crack of the door that led to the dining room. The furniture wax smell vanished instantly.

But Lydia had no one to help her.

"Rosy, why don't *you* help Lydia with questions?" Robin liked Lydia and felt sorry that the girl didn't have a mother around. "It's Rosy's birthday on Thursday, but we're having her party on Sunday – I have Sunday off this week." Robin put an arm around Lydia. "We'd love it if you could come – but no presents. We're having our neighbors in for potluck. Our friend, Mr. Spinelli, is bringing a cake for his wife, too, so there will be plenty to go around."

"Oh, I'd love to! My birthday is on Saturday. A few girls I know from school are coming over in the afternoon. Can you come, Rosy?" Lydia hoped she would, but Rosy thought she'd rather have her teeth drilled.

"Uh, no thanks. I won't have time. I've really got to put a costume together."

As they went to leave, Tiffany opened up again. "Well, look for me on the six o'clock news. Tonight I'm beginning a new series on local athletes…should be good." She threw her hand over her mouth. "Oh, that's right, Lydia said you don't have…uh, I mean…you don't watch television."

That was the moment when Rosy realized that Lydia really needed her help.

Chapter 9

Rosy got off the bus at her usual stop, leaving her mom to go to work. She headed for the library, where she was greeted by Helen, who was on her break.

"Hello, dear. Hot, isn't it? Okay, here's one for you." Rosy could tell she'd been waiting to ask the question. "What color was the dress with puffed sleeves that Matthew gave Anne?" She took a swig from her teacup and looked anxiously at Rosy.

"That's an easy one, Helen. It was brown." Rosy knew she was expecting her to say blue, because Anne tells Matthew in Chapter 2 that she imagines herself in a beautiful, pale blue silk dress.

"That's right." Helen was disappointed she hadn't

managed to stump Rosy. "I thought you'd say blue. Everyone says blue. It was blue in the movie version."

"Well, in the book it was soft brown gloria – whatever that is – and had frills and shirring and a ruffle of filmy lace at the neck. And Mrs. Lynde gave her a brown hair ribbon to match." Rosy was thinking that since all the other competitors had likely been weaned on the video version, they might be tripped up on such a question. She was about to ask Helen for another one when a booming voice came from behind her.

"Oh…Rosa. Show me how to use the computer – the Internet – will you?" It was Mr. Spinelli, wearing overalls spattered with white paint. He had a loaf of bread under one arm. "I've only got a second. My wife won't let me take a break from painting, but I'm worried about my car." His wife's sister was coming for a visit to celebrate Mrs. Spinelli's birthday, and Mrs. S. wanted the whole place painted before the weekend. House, fence, everything. "Nobody around here has the parts for my car, and I've got to find someone who does!"

"Come over here," Rosy said. Mr. Spinelli grabbed a pen from the table, and while Rosy scanned the search results for wreckers and auto parts dealers, he wrote down the numbers on the palm of his hand. "You're an angel from heaven, Rosa!" He picked her up and hugged her so hard that one of Lydia's Life Savers sprang out of her mouth. And his loaf of bread was never the same again.

"Oh, by the way...Mr. Spinelli..." Rosy thought it was a good time to ask about the car. "I was wondering if my brother Ben – you know, the one who is going to be a doctor and who is so careful and responsible otherwise no one would ever let him take out their appendix – well I was hoping maybe you would let him borrow your Pontiac for the day and it *is* a Sunday and you know how light the traffic is on Sundays, so I could go to Rockton for the Anne of Green Gables look-alike contest." She took a minute to breathe. "You see, it is the only way I will win the boxed set of books and you are my only hope."

"Rosa, Rosa, Rosa. I am your only hope?" He looked at the ceiling. "And this is the only way you'll win the books?" He looked at the floor. Then he thought for a minute or two, and finally agreed to her request.

But not without a speech about the dangers involved in driving such an old car. "I don't have much insurance on my car, Rosa, because I do not drive anywhere except church and the market. You must promise that the car will not be driven fast. Do you understand, Rosa?"

Rosy assured Mr. Spinelli they'd be careful, especially since he'd finally gotten the car door back on. Ben would be exceptionally cautious, stay on the back roads, and be home early, long before dark.

"I hope I can find the parts!" Mr. Spinelli yelled as he made a beeline across the street. Traffic in both directions came to a screeching halt.

"Not half as much as I do!" Rosy muttered.

Rosy spent another hour at the library, then went over to Jay and Sebastian's. She told them the whole story about Tiffany and the doctor.

"Lydia told me that Tiffany puts on a big act about liking her, but actually wishes her father had no daughter." She picked up a piece of brick that had broken away from the foundation behind the steps and shoved it back in. "She doesn't even *pretend* to like me."

"Well, I think it's terrible how she's been to you and that poor little Anne look-alike!" Sebastian was genuinely upset.

"Don't call her that!" exclaimed Rosy. "*I'm* going to win this contest. I have to! Anyhow, a lot of it has to do with portrayal of personality, and Lydia doesn't really have a personality."

Sebastian laughed and said, "Of course she does. Everyone has a personality of some sort." Then he turned to Rosy. "So why is Lydia entering the contest?"

"To find out if her dad loves her. I don't know if he does or not. It's hard to tell." Rosy gave them each a Life Saver and took one herself. "I had to seize these, to save Lydia from herself." Rosy sat down on the step. "Say, can you guys sew?"

"Still no costume?" questioned Jay.

"I can't find anything that will do. I don't want anything fancy, just a very ugly yellowish-gray dress, a faded brown sailor hat, a carpetbag, and a wig of red braids. The rich girls will be decked out in gingham and flowers. And *that's* where they'll make their first mistake."

"No problem getting you a wig, Rosy. There's an old red one at the salon we can braid. The owner won't even miss it," said Sebastian, popping the candy into his mouth. "Mmm. I'd forgotten how good these are."

"We don't sew," added Jay, "but Mrs. Rodrigues does, and her hair needs re-coloring, so maybe we can work something out with her."

Rosy, tired of searching in vain for a costume, was relieved things seemed to be falling in place. She insisted on cleaning Jay and Sebastian's place for Mrs. Rodrigues, to make up for sewing the dress. All she needed now was the fabric.

"Did you say yellowish-gray?" inquired Sebastian, resting his chin in his hand. "Matilda, our boss at The Tangerine, just put up new curtains. The ones she took down – you know, Jay, those pale gray linen ones – well, they were lovely in their day, but hours and hours in the sun have turned them an ugly yellow color. They might do the trick!"

"But she's stingy, Seb. She'll want to be paid for them even if they *are* ready for the garbage! They weren't cheap, either. I think the linen was imported." Jay looked at Rosy. She handed him another candy.

"Maybe I could do some odd jobs for her – sweep up hair or something." Rosy was determined.

Before Jay could respond, Mr. Spinelli's voice came thundering from across the street.

"Rosa! Rosa! I've found a place that has what I need, but I have to get there tomorrow." He stopped talking for a second, lowered both eyebrows, then grimaced. "If I don't get these parts, you won't get to Rockville."

"Rockton, Mr. Spinelli."

Mr. Spinelli sat down next to Rosy, and she gave him a Life Saver to calm him down. "My wife is going to make me paint all day. She'll kill me if I don't finish the place by Saturday, but I must get the parts."

He'd made a list: all he needed was a brake line, brake shoes, radiator hose, radiator hose clamps, water pump, starter switch, fuel pump, ignition wires, and an ignition switch – and then his car would run like new.

"My friend, Battista, he'll take me tomorrow to get the parts. Lucia, she'll be out all day shopping. Spending money! All for her sister! I'll go with Battista, if you can paint the fence. Then I'll finish the house by Saturday."

Rosy took the brush out of his hand and agreed to help him get the job done. "Don't you worry, Mr. Spinelli. You can count on me. I'll have the fence done tomorrow, and that'll give you three days to finish the rest."

So, it was settled. She had a ride to Rockton, and a costume – almost. All she had to do was paint a fence, sweep up hair at The Tangerine, and clean Jay and Sebastian's place. Everything was coming together. That boxed set would soon be hers.

Chapter 10

The next day, Rosy got up, put on an old shirt from the ragbag, and watched out the window for Mrs. Spinelli to leave to go shopping. The minute she'd disappeared down the alley, Mr. Spinelli emerged from the front door, looked in both directions twice, then signaled for Rosy to come over.

He stuck a painter's cap on Rosy's head, then handed her a bucket of enamel and a brush.

"Don't worry, Mr. Spinelli. Everything will go fine." Rosy waved as he scrambled into his friend's car (which didn't appear to be in much better condition than the Pontiac) and sped off down the street.

Other than the excessive heat and humidity, and soaring

pollution levels that nearly flattened her, Rosy made out quite nicely with the fence. About an hour into the job, Jay came by on his way to work to check how she was doing.

"Looks pretty good there, Rosy-girl!" He gave her a glass of water, sent by Robin, who reminded Rosy constantly to drink water in the heat. "I called Matilda," Jay said, "and she's agreed to let you have the fabric if you'll work for her for an hour or so on Saturday morning. She wants the aromatherapy bottles filled, and needs someone with small hands to do it."

"Great!" replied Rosy, gulping down the water. "And Mrs. Rodrigues?"

"She's on board, too. We'll bring the curtains home today and she'll take your measurements tonight after dinner. You can tell her exactly what you want." He took the empty glass. "Good luck with the fence!"

And so the day went: her brothers brought her more water and even helped a bit, her mother handed her a sandwich on her way to work, and various neighborhood kids stopped by to gawk. Six hours, seven glasses of water, and eleven Life Savers later, Rosy was finished. And it looked good, except for the paint she had spilled on the grass when she kicked Patrick for running his finger along the top rail to see if it was dry. By three o'clock, she was done painting forever.

Just as she was banging the lid back on the can, the car carrying Mr. Spinelli came blasting into the drive and out he jumped. He yelled some things to his friend Battista, who sped off once again. In a bag was some kind of car part, but it wasn't a brake line, brake shoes, radiator hose, radiator hose clamps, water pump, starter switch, fuel pump, ignition wires, and ignition switch.

"Oh, Rosa! They had nothing there. Just the starter switch, and that's it! They told me my car's too old to find the parts. Can you imagine that? Too old to find the parts? Well, I won't give up." He looked at the fence. "Oh! Wonderful, Rosa. You're an angel from heaven."

Then, through the corner of his eye, he spotted Mrs. Spinelli coming down the street and broke into damage control mode. He pulled the painter's cap off Rosy's head, grabbed the brush, and flung paint onto his face. He even rubbed some on the seat of his pants, because he never failed to back into wet paint and that would be the first place his wife would look if she suspected anything. Then he gave a performance that could have won him an Academy Award.

"Yes, Rosa, you are right. I did a beautiful job on the fence. But nothing is too good for my Lucia. She wants everything nice for her sister." He pretended to be surprised by his wife's arrival. "Lucia! You back so soon?"

"Well, I'd better be going," said Rosy. "Nice talking to

you. Bye, Mrs. Spinelli. I guess I'll see you at our party on Sunday!" But Mrs. S. was too busy examining the fence, so Rosy went home and flaked out. The heat was getting to her, and the paint fumes were aggravating. She thought about going to the library to relax in the air-conditioning, but it was almost closing time.

After less than five minutes on the couch, she heard a knock at the door. It was Mr. Spinelli, who – since he still needed a brake line, brake shoes, radiator hose, radiator hose clamps, water pump, fuel pump, ignition wires, and ignition switch – had to try another parts dealer the next day. Because his wife had more shopping to do for her sister's visit, Rosy once again agreed to fill in. This time, it was the porch she'd have to paint.

Wednesday. Sky-high smog levels. Four hours of painting. Ben stopped by in Mr. Wing's delivery car and reminded her that if she didn't drink a lot, she would soon collapse. He grabbed the brush from her hand and attacked the porch.

"You're going to be a good doctor, you know," declared Rosy, taking a gulp from his water bottle.

"I'll never make it to university, Rosy. I haven't got the money, you know that."

"Well, you've got the marks!" Rosy slapped the brush down on the porch.

"I've applied, but there's just no way. I'm trying to find another job to help Mom – I mean, besides delivering Chinese food, which is what I should be doing now. Mr. Wing has another delivery ready for me." Rosy wished there was something she could do to help him. Like her, his life (as Anne would say) was "a graveyard of buried hopes."

"You're a hard worker, Ben," said Rosy, setting the brush on top of the can. "You're not like our father, that's for sure."

"Oh, Dad wasn't all bad, Rosy. It's a shame you never had the chance to spend any time with him." Ben wiped a drop of paint from his sister's cheek. "I think he must regret not knowing his daughter."

"It was his choice, Ben."

"I guess. But life sometimes makes choices for us." He turned to leave, then stopped. "You know that old baseball of mine? That was his father's. When he gave it to me, he told me that I would play in the big league one day." Ben smiled. "And I believed him, Rosy. I believed him."

Rosy didn't speak.

"Did you know that our grandfather was the best pitcher in the city?" added Ben. "Dad said he could strike guys out blindfolded and with one arm tied behind his back."

"No, I didn't know that," said Rosy quietly. "But now I know why you won't let anyone touch that ball."

Mr. Spinelli arrived as Ben was leaving, and had with him one ignition switch and a brake line. He still needed brake shoes, a radiator hose and clamps, a water pump, a fuel pump, and ignition wires. Unless he got them, Rosy wasn't going to make it to Rockton, and Mrs. Rodrigues had taken her measurements and everything. She had promised to sew a marvelously ugly yellowish-gray dress, and Rosy couldn't wait to show all those rich girls that she – *she* – was the closest thing to Anne of Green Gables they'd ever meet.

Thursday. Her twelfth birthday. Complete exhaustion. She finished painting the porch while Mrs. Spinelli shopped and Mr. Spinelli made a third trip for parts. He came back with everything except the radiator hose and water pump, but he decided to repair the old ones. Finally, the car was good enough to be driven.

Friday. Bone tired, but delighted that Mrs. Rodrigues was working on the costume and had even devised a carpet-bag for "Anne" to carry. Rosy cleaned her way through Jay and Sebastian's place: she vacuumed the living room carpet, polished the bathroom sink and tub, washed the kitchen floor, and dusted everything she could find with spray wax. She straightened up their magazine rack, washed the windows, and made the place shine. It would be smooth sailing from that point on.

On Saturday morning, Rosy took the bus downtown to

The Tangerine Coiffure and waited outside for the owner to arrive. She was beat from the previous few days, but as this was her last task, she felt good about being on the home stretch. At half past nine, Matilda pulled up in a fancy car.

"Oh, hello. You must be Jay and Sebastian's friend. Well, come in. Make yourself at home, and I'll show you what I need done." She opened the door and threw her silk scarf onto a coat rack. Rosy was relieved the place was air-conditioned.

"What I need you to do is fill all these small vials with the essential oils, which are kept stored in these larger bottles. Now, please keep in mind that these are costly plant derivatives. The ylang-ylang, when blended with rose, is several hundred dollars an ounce, so we have to be very careful not to spill any of it. I don't want to scare you, I just want you to take your time. I'd do this myself, but I need someone with steady hands and perfect eyesight."

She checked her reflection in the mirror and pushed her long mane behind her ears. "Any minute now, my clients will begin to arrive, so it would be better if you could work in the back room. Is that okay?"

"Sure, no problem." Rosy just wanted to get the job done. "How much did you say that ylang stuff was?"

Matilda put a bottle of liquid in front of her on the table. "This would be about fifty dollars." Then she put a second bottle, smaller still, next to the first one. "This is the blend with rose. It's worth ten times that."

Rosy started by getting out all the big bottles and placing them carefully on the table in front of her. There was patchouli, rose, bitter orange, sweet orange, orange blossom, sandalwood, cedarwood, lavender, jasmine, neroli, lemongrass, palmarosa, petitgrain, tea tree, cinnamon, chamomile, clary sage and – of course – the omnipresent ylang-ylang. All the smells combined left Rosy feeling as if her nose had been taken hostage by a mad French perfume maker.

When customers began to show up, she listened as they gave instructions as to how they wanted their hair cut and their nails manicured and their skin exfoliated. She wished her mother could have her skin exfoliated – whatever that was. She wished her mother could afford to boss people around. She wished her mother didn't have to spend every penny she earned on food and rent.

As she filled vials, imagining what she'd buy her mother one day when she became a famous stage actress, she detected a familiar smell. A smell so powerful it smothered even the ylang-ylang blend she'd finally found the nerve to pour. "What *is* that smell?" she asked herself.

When she realized it was chlorine with a twist of cologne, the bottle of oil slipped right out of her hand.

Chapter 11

Rosy figured the fact she caught it before more than a few drops fell had probably saved her from a jail sentence, since she could never have repaid that kind of money.

Seeing as the smidgen of ylang-ylang that she did spill probably cost at least twenty dollars, Rosy wiped it up fast and wiped it out of her mind forever. What she couldn't erase was the fact that Tiffany was in the next room. Rosy wasn't in the mood for another confrontation.

Tiffany, completely relaxed in a lounge chair and propped up with overstuffed velvet cushions, had a steaming white towel over her face (thank heavens) and a woman working away at her nails.

Rosy listened as she rambled on to the manicurist.

"Tricia, you're going to have to work faster. I've got to be at the stadium by noon to get an interview with that new coach. I don't even have time for my highlights today, but I'll need them done soon." Then she muttered something about meeting Lydia's father that evening.

Considering her options, Rosy thought it best to stay out of sight, finish filling the vials, then disappear when Tiffany was looking in the other direction.

She had just put away the last bottle when Matilda called her into the next room – the room in which Tiffany was having a mud-pack glopped onto her face. "Do you mind cleaning up this mess for me? You'll find a mop and pail in the closet...right over there."

The mess to which she referred was the goo that had dropped off Tiffany's face. Since there was still a towel covering Tiffany, Rosy reckoned she'd clean up the mud quickly, then get out of sight once and for all.

Suddenly she heard Tiffany say, "Her dad will love it if I help her win. I'm going to do everything I can to see that Lydia does win this Anne contest. She's certainly homely enough. That Indian girl doesn't stand a chance. I can't imagine an aboriginal Anne."

Rosy's chin dropped and her heart thumped inside her chest like it was a bass drum.

The manicurist finished with Tiffany's nails and signaled for another woman to continue on her face. Once Tiffany had cucumber slices on her eyes, Rosy figured she'd better get out of the salon while the going was good.

She wasn't sure if a person could see through cucumber slices or not and didn't want to take any chances. So she snatched a towel from the storage room, put it over her head, and waited for an opportunity to escape without being seen. When the phone rang, and Matilda went to answer it, Rosy made a mad dash for the front door and down the street.

All the way home on the bus, Rosy thought about what Tiffany had said about her. That she didn't have a prayer when it came to winning the contest.

For a minute, Rosy wondered if she was right.

Maybe it was the silliest thing on earth: a Native girl believing she could be Anne of Green Gables.

Maybe she'd make a complete fool out of herself.

Maybe everyone would laugh at her.

But why should they laugh? Anne is supposed to have as many shades as a rainbow, so why couldn't she be Anne?

She *could* be Anne.

She could win the contest.

Even if Tiffany did help Lydia.

But to make sure she'd win, she'd have to continue working on those questions with Helen. She stopped by the library and spent a few hours there, enlisting the librarian's help whenever she had a spare minute, and trying not to think about the sportscaster.

By closing time, Helen assured Rosy she could not think of a single question the judges might throw at her that she couldn't answer. As far as the librarian was concerned, at least in terms of knowledge of the books, Rosy had the thing nailed.

Rosy didn't feel well when she got up on Sunday, having tossed and turned all night thinking about what Tiffany had said. The factories were busy churning out their usual fumes, and the smog was at its usual record levels, but Rosy was ready to enjoy her party nevertheless, despite having to use her inhaler twice before noon.

"Rosy," said her mother, "I think you've done too much all week." Robin worried constantly about her and Patrick in the hot weather.

"Just another week in Steeltown." But with the work behind her and their home bedecked with balloons and streamers, Rosy looked forward to a fun day with the neighbors. Her mother had baked a chocolate cake with white icing and had written on it "Happy Birthday Rosy" and stuck twelve candles on top.

"Hey, Mom," asked Rosy, "can a person see through cucumber slices?"

"I don't know," replied Robin. "There's one in the fridge from Mrs. Spinelli's garden." Rosy headed for the kitchen. "Why does it matter?"

While she was slicing the cucumber, Rosy thought about Lydia's party and wondered how it had gone. She'd never been to a rich kid's party, but imagined there'd be a lot of bows involved – bows on the gifts brought by friends wearing bows, bows on the walls and on the staircase railing, bows on everything and everyone. And maybe there'd be an orchestra. Or a string quartet.

Just as she was sticking cucumbers on her eyes, John yelled from the front window, "Here she comes!" A big yellow cab pulled up, and the driver got out and opened the back door for Lydia. Rosy detested the whole taxi routine, while her brother found it fascinating. "She's carrying something in a box! It's huge!"

"I told her no presents," said Robin. "I hope she didn't buy something." Rosy hoped she did buy something.

"Glad you could come, Lydia." Robin welcomed the girl inside. "Rosy's friends from school will be here a bit later. We're going to have Mrs. Spinelli's cake first. Her husband should be along with it any minute now."

"Speaking of cakes," sighed Lydia, "I brought mine with me." She opened up the box, and inside was the grandest, flashiest, hugest, most garish cake Rosy had ever seen in her whole life. It had three tiers, like a wedding cake, and "Happy Birthday Lydia" was inscribed across the top. The writing must have been done by a professional calligrapher, it was so smooth and even.

Rosy looked at the cake her mom had made; "Happy" looked pretty good, but by the time she'd written "Birthday," the last four letters were squeezed in to fit, getting smaller and smaller and smaller. The "osy" of "Rosy" plunged right over the side.

But it was her mom's handwriting.

It was perfect.

Chapter 12

"Why didn't you have your cake yesterday, at your party?" asked Rosy.

"None of the girls from school could come. The MacLeods are at their summer home, the Kowalskis have left for Bermuda, and Jessica Richards had a riding lesson." Lydia looked down at her feet. "My father was at the hospital all day, and I was asleep by the time he got back."

Rosy glanced at Lydia. She couldn't help but feel sorry for her.

"And Tiffany was at the stadium, covering the exhibition game. Anyway she wouldn't touch a piece of cake even if you paid her," Lydia continued.

"She doesn't eat cake?" asked Patrick, examining the

magnificent one Lydia had brought. "What, is she crazy or something?"

"Crazy like a fox," murmured Rosy.

"What?" asked Lydia.

Ben walked into the room, causing Lydia to trip over the foot of the sofa. She fell forward, landed in his arms, and turned a shade of red that Rosy'd never seen in her life. Embarrassed, she pulled out her Life Savers and offered him one.

"That's a beautiful cake," he said, taking a candy. "Do we all get a slice?"

"I thought you'd given up these things," said Rosy sharply, as she confiscated two unopened rolls from Lydia's pocket.

Rosy didn't get a chance to ask any more questions about Tiffany, since the neighbors were arriving. Mrs. Rodrigues brought in a dozen Portuguese *papo-secos*, the most delicious crusty rolls one could ever taste, and Mr. and Mrs. Wing supplied cartons of Chinese food.

Jay and Sebastian asked Lydia if she was ready for the contest and wanted to know what kind of a costume she had planned.

"I don't know yet. My father's girlfriend ordered it directly from Prince Edward Island – from a woman who works for the Charlottetown Festival." Lydia shrugged her shoulders. "I don't know why Tiffany's being so nice to me. She usually can't stand to be around me. She even offered to ask me questions to prepare for the contest."

Rosy grimaced. Then she bit her tongue. She was tempted to spill the beans, and tell everyone what Tiffany was up to.

"You mean from a professional designer?" inquired Jay.

"She sews costumes for the *Anne of Green Gables* musical. I saw it twice when it came here." Lydia answered their questions in a matter-of-fact kind of way. She wasn't trying to brag, but the fact she had seen the musical really bugged Rosy. Even more than the costume.

Rosy didn't care about movies. Her aspiration was to become a stage actress. To see a live theater production would be the experience of a lifetime for Rosy. It wasn't fair that Lydia got to see the musical twice, while Rosy couldn't even afford a seat in the back row next to the bathrooms.

Rosy asked herself why she ever became involved with this girl in the first place; but then she *was* still Plan B, given the shaky condition of the Pontiac.

"Okay," said Rosy defiantly. "You know what we're going to do? Lydia and I will recite the readings that we've prepared for the contest."

"We will?" asked Lydia.

Rosy wanted to show everyone that she had genuine

acting ability – something no Virgo could ever have. Even if she had seen the musical ten times. And even if she did have a tailor-made costume.

As Rosy was about to begin, Mr. Spinelli came crashing through the door.

"My wife, she's going to kill me. She's going to kill me this time for sure." Robin made him sit on the couch and asked John to get him a glass of ginger-ale punch.

"I've been so busy with my car all week, and painting, and picking up Lucia's sister at the bus terminal, I forgot to get her cake! She doesn't have a cake! They're on their way here now." He jumped up and looked out the window. "Oh, no! Here she comes! What will I do?"

Rosy thought fast. She grabbed Lydia by the back of her dress and pulled her aside.

"Can I have your cake?"

"My cake?"

"Your cake. Can I have it?"

"I guess so." Lydia didn't know what Rosy had in mind until she watched her take her finger, wipe the "y" and the "d" out of "Lydia," then dig a "u" and a "c" into the icing.

"There. 'Happy Birthday Lucia.' Thanks, Lydia." Rosy set the massive cake on the coffee table in front of Mr. Spinelli, who, when he saw it, picked her up in the air and hugged her so tight, she almost passed out.

"Rosa! My Rosa! You're an angel from heaven!"

It took Rosy a full minute to get the air back into her lungs. "Don't thank me, Mr. Spinelli. It was Lydia's cake. She's the one you should be thanking."

"Lydia. A beautiful name, Lydia." He threw *her* up in the air, too. "You know what you are, Lydia? You know what you are? You're a real *lifesaver!*"

"You can say that again!" declared Rosy, opening the door for Mrs. Spinelli and her sister.

"Ciao! Hello. Ciao!" exclaimed Mrs. Spinelli. "Happy Birthday, Rosa!"

"Grazie. Happy Birthday to you too, Mrs. Spinelli!"

"How old are you now?"

"Twelve – like you!" joked Rosy, and Mrs. Spinelli and her sister laughed.

When Mrs. Spinelli got a look at her gorgeous cake, she was astounded, and stared at it like it was the first time she'd ever seen a cake in her life. (No one in the room, save Lydia, *had* ever seen one like that.) Mr. Spinelli sat with a foolish grin on his face and didn't say a word. He was afraid she'd ask him where he bought it.

After the shock wore off, Mrs. Spinelli's interrogation began, but it was in Italian.

Fear came over Mr. Spinelli's face again and he turned to Rosy. "My beautiful Lucia, she wants to know why the middle of her name is wiped out."

Rosy remained nonchalant. "I'm sorry. The cake looked so lovely, I simply had to taste it."

So Mrs. Spinelli got up, stomped over to the table on which Rosy's cake sat, took her finger and smudged out the middle of Rosy's name. Then she walked back to the sofa, laughed and said, "Well, I just had to taste your cake, too!"

Sebastian stepped in quickly. "Okay, girls, let's hear your presentations. You go first, Lydia."

"Well, I've decided to sing a song from the musical." Her bony hands trembled, and she turned as white as the inside of one of Mrs. Rodrigues's buns. She focused her eyes over the top of everyone's heads, and Rosy knew she was pretending they were in their underwear again.

Lydia stood up and in a high-pitched voice sang "Gee, I'm Glad I'm No One Else but Me." The only one smiling was Mr. Spinelli, who bobbed his head and moved his fingers back and forth like a conductor throughout the entire thing. Everybody else looked like they'd swallowed an ice-cold drink too quickly and had brain-freeze.

"That was quite nice, Lydia," said Robin, passing around paper cups of punch. "And you certainly remind me of Anne." Everyone in the room agreed. Rosy knew they were just relieved the song didn't have a fourth verse.

"My turn," said Rosy. She didn't care if she looked like

Anne or not – her spirit would shine through. Rosy paused for a minute, looked up at the ceiling, then recited her piece.

Her rendition was so piercing, so poignant, that it went straight to the heart. Her friends and family could feel – they could touch – the bravery of the orphan, waiting at that station, so grateful to finally belong to someone.

Rosy glanced around the room and could tell she had everyone's undivided attention. Jay was biting his knuckle to stop himself from tearing up.

She continued, but stopped when she sensed the room spinning. She was lightheaded and her breathing was shallow. Her neighbors' faces began to swim before her, and she felt as if she was drowning. She started to wheeze uncontrollably.

Then, not at all.

"Quick! Ben! Get Rosy's inhaler! It's up in her room." Robin rushed to her daughter's side and held her head upright. The inhaler didn't help. Her lips were turning blue. Nothing would stop the attack.

The previous week had been too much. The work. The smog. The heat. The paint. The spray wax. Ylang-ylang. Two hugs from Mr. Spinelli in less than seven days.

Rosy couldn't breathe. Everything happened so fast, she had no time to think. And yet, for some reason, the contest came into her mind and she worried that if she was to drop dead, she'd never win the set of books.

Mr. Spinelli ran across the street to get the Pontiac. He tried to start the car, but the motor was dead. John flung open the hood, jostled the ignition wires into place, and within a minute, the engine turned over. Ben carried Rosy to the car, and Robin drove with them to the hospital, which was, thankfully, just around the corner.

Rosy drifted into unconsciousness.

Chapter 13

When she woke up, she was in a hospital room, and standing around her were her mother, a nurse, Ben, John, Patrick, Mrs. Spinelli, Mrs. Spinelli's sister, Mrs. Rodrigues, Jay and Sebastian, and the Wings. They were all chewing Mrs. Spinelli's cake from paper towels. Lydia and Mr. Spinelli were so shaken by Rosy's seizure that the nurse had made them lie down on two of the spare beds in the ward.

"Are they okay?" Rosy asked her mother once she'd remembered what had happened.

"They'll be fine, but you need to rest. And don't talk so much." She held a straw to Rosy's mouth so she could sip water. "You had a bad attack, and because Dr. Levy fears it could trigger a second wave, you've got to stay here for at least a week."

"A week? No!" said Rosy, furiously. As a veteran asthmatic, she was well acquainted with the so-called second wave. She often had to be kept in hospital so the doctors could give her medication intravenously to reduce the swelling in her air tubes. "Oh, Mom, please tell Dr. Levy I have to go to the contest on Sunday. She'll understand. I'll be real good all week, and I won't move a muscle." Rosy pleaded with Robin. "Besides, the contest is exactly a week away, so there's a chance I'll get out in time. Isn't there?"

"Rosy, your health is more important than any contest."

Mrs. Spinelli, Mrs. Spinelli's sister, Mr. and Mrs. Wing, Mrs. Rodrigues, Jay, and Sebastian all agreed. John and Patrick were fooling around with the oxygen mask that hung beside Rosy, and Ben was attending to Mr. Spinelli and Lydia. The nurse told everyone they had to leave shortly so Rosy could rest.

Rosy didn't say a word. She told herself that if she had to tie sheets together and rappel down the side of the building, she would make it to the contest. Period.

After they'd gone (Mr. Spinelli and Lydia had to be wheeled out), the nurse admitted another patient into the room. The teenager was given the bed next to Rosy, who struck up a conversation despite feeling like she could sleep for a year.

"Welcome to Ward 12A," said Rosy. "So what are you here for?"

"Broken bones. Rollerblading." Rosy knew from experience that people in beds either chatter all day nonstop so you can't get a word in edgewise with a shoehorn, or they speak in syllables. This girl, whose name was Gwen, fell into the second category.

So Rosy was destined to spend a whole week with someone she didn't know, trying to think of something to say when she didn't feel like saying anything at all.

Only the food was worse than that prospect. But at least, being vegetarian, Rosy didn't have to face any disgusting type of hospital-prepared meat. And her mom had brought over her birthday cake, which she and Gwen ate bit by bit all week long.

After the second day, Rosy was feeling well enough to make a to-do list.

1. Ask Mrs. Rodrigues to come by and fit the costume, so she can make any necessary alterations.
2. Ask Mom to bring over my *Anne* book so that I can go through it with a fine tooth comb.
3. Devise and implement a strategy to prevent Tiffany from doing anything to ruin my chances of winning the contest.

There was no problem with the first two items. Mrs. Rodrigues delivered the yellowish-gray wincey dress and when Rosy tried it on, it fit perfectly. The unsightly carpet-bag completed the costume nicely.

Her mother brought several *Anne* books that Helen had checked out of the library for her. (Helen didn't want her to have to rely on the copy with thirty-seven pages missing.)

"She also sent a little gift for you, Rosy," said Robin. "She told me it wasn't much, but that you would know exactly what it meant."

Robin handed Rosy a small, gift-wrapped box with a note attached. It said: "Hope you're feeling better soon. Good luck on Sunday." Rosy removed the paper carefully (her mother always saved wrapping paper). Inside was a brand-new green felt pen. And she knew exactly what it meant.

"It means Helen knows I'm going to win the boxed set. That's what it means."

"*If* you are well enough to make it, Rosy," reminded Robin. "And right now that is certainly not the case."

About an hour after her mom had left, Lydia arrived with a huge bouquet of silk flowers. "I thought maybe real ones would be bad for your asthma," she said, bumping into the edge of the bedside table. "My mother loved flowers and used to fill the house with them all year round. Before she left."

"Thanks, Lydia." Rosy didn't know what to say about her mom. It was obvious how much Lydia missed her. "You're right about my asthma – those plant oils at The Tangerine nearly finished me."

"Have you been to The Tangerine? Tiffany goes there all the time. What were you doing there?"

Realizing she'd almost blown it, Rosy changed the subject fast. She didn't want Tiffany to find out she'd been there, listening. Lydia might let it slip.

"Your mother, she's British, isn't she?"

"Oh yes, she's from Yorkshire. Well, she was born there, and then she went to school in London, and that's where she met my father." Lydia fiddled with the flowers.

"I guess she missed living in England." Rosy figured she was homesick, and that's why she had left.

Lydia bit her lower lip. "She said there's nothing here for her. Not really."

"Why didn't you go to England with your mom?" Rosy couldn't understand why Lydia stayed in Hamilton.

"Well," replied Lydia, "my mother has a big family and lots of friends there. Dad has nobody but me." The two girls locked eyes for a second, then Lydia looked away. "He has a brother in Canmore, Alberta, but they don't keep in touch."

Rosy wasn't sure how to respond. "So have you been practicing for the contest?"

Gwen shut off the television. The girls' conversation was better than the soap operas she'd been watching.

Lydia hesitated. "Tiffany hired a professional singing coach for me, Rosy."

"That's nice," was her reply. She told herself it wouldn't help anyway.

Rosy, whose nose was beginning to work, sniffed and sniffed again, then blurted out, "Cherry Life Savers! Aha!" Then she reached into Lydia's bag and pulled out several unopened rolls, and one that was half-eaten. "Okay, Lydia, you're busted." She threw a couple of rolls to Gwen, then put the rest in the drawer.

That's when Lydia jumped out of her chair and bolted into the hall.

"Dad!" she hollered. "Hi Dad! I thought you were at the university today—"

"Quiet, Lydia," he scolded. "You're in a hospital, for heaven's sake." He opened up a file and starting reading, ignoring his daughter completely. Rosy felt embarrassed for her.

"Can I drive home with you?" pleaded Lydia. "I don't mind waiting."

"No. I won't be home until late tonight." He kept on reading, then put his hand into his pocket and pulled out a twenty-dollar bill. Without even taking his eyes from the file, he handed it to his daughter and told her to take a cab.

Lydia glanced into Rosy's room.

Rosy pretended she hadn't heard any of it, and struck up a conversation with Gwen (which was no easy task).

It worked until Lydia stepped backward into an elderly patient coming behind her with an IV stand.

Crash!

"Oh, Lydia," rebuked the doctor.

"I'm sorry," mumbled Lydia. "I'm sorry, Dad."

"You're such a…such a…" While he attended to the patient, the red-faced girl ran off down the hall.

Rosy went to go after her but was stopped in her tracks by a horrific stabbing pain in her chest. She got herself back into bed, and not a minute too soon. Dr. Levy arrived to take more tests and had she seen that, there would have been no chance that Rosy'd be released in time for the contest. Rosy used every bit of willpower she had to fight back a cough.

Luckily, Dr. Levy's attention was diverted when Robin and Ben came through the door. Rosy introduced her oldest brother as "the one who's going to be a fabulous physician," prompting him to speak up.

"Rosy knows I can't afford to go to university, but she never stops telling people I'm going to be a doctor," he said quietly.

Lydia's father walked in and handed a stack of papers to Dr. Levy. He didn't seem the slightest bit worried about Lydia, and Rosy felt like screaming at him.

Dr. Levy spoke to Ben. "Are you aware of the various scholarships available for aboriginal students – especially if they want to pursue a career in medicine?"

Robin interjected. "He is not a full status Indian because I left the reserve and married a – well, his father is not Indian."

The doctor persisted. "If I am not mistaken, there may be bursaries available for non-status Indians. If you want, I could check into this for you. Your sister tells me your marks are excellent."

Rosy wanted to get in on the conversation, but her chest was tight, and she had to focus on breathing. But when no one accepted the doctor's offer, she was compelled to speak. "We'd be grateful if you did that for us."

"Rosy!" protested Robin. "Dr. Levy is a busy woman. We can't expect her to—"

"No," added Ben, "I can't ask you to do that for me. I spoke to my teacher, but he didn't know much about funding for aboriginals and said I'd likely have to pay half the tuition myself. And he told me I'd need to do volunteer work in a hospital. I've asked for a job, but without experience, they won't take me on – even as a volunteer."

"It would certainly help if you could get practical experience," said Lydia's father.

"Well, let me see what I can find out," offered Dr. Levy, as she left with Dr. Parker to discuss something with a nurse in the hallway. "Rosy, you can visit with your family for a few minutes, but I'll be back soon to run those tests."

Once her mother and Ben were gone, Rosy called Lydia's father back into her room. He was finished talking with the nurse, and she didn't want him to get away.

"Anything wrong?" he asked.

"No, no," replied Rosy. "Well, not with me anyway." She had to stop for a minute to catch her breath.

"Yes?"

"Well," she said, "I know that you're a heart specialist, and that means you know a lot about hearts and everything. But, well…I might as well jump right to the point." She cleared her throat. "You're going to break Lydia's if you don't show up at the contest." Then she really threw caution to the wind. "And it wouldn't be the first time."

Chapter 14

It was Thursday before Rosy was able to work on her third goal of the week: to devise and implement a strategy to prevent Tiffany from doing anything on the day of the contest to ruin her chances of winning. It was a visit from Jay and Sebastian that proved to be the break she was waiting for.

They arrived with a red wig, which they'd braided flawlessly, but when Rosy tried it on she looked very weird.

"Are you ready for the contest?" asked Jay, who couldn't help laughing at the sight of Rosy in long braids.

"Will you be able to go?" added Sebastian.

"Yes, I'm ready and if all goes well, I'll be sprung by the weekend. Otherwise, I'm busting out of here, trust me."

Rosy removed the wig and from the tone of her voice, the two fellows knew she had a serious request. "I need your help. I wouldn't ask you guys, but I can't do this on my own."

Gwen shut the television off again, and Rosy advised Jay and Sebastian that they were free to talk in front of Gwen. Then she told them the whole story about what happened at The Tangerine, and why Tiffany wanted Lydia to win.

"That's awful," cried Jay. "What do you think she'll do? Turn the judges against you?"

"No," replied Rosy, "because she doesn't think I have a hope of winning. But she'll do everything she can to see that Lydia wins, so she can look good to Lydia's dad."

"So where do we come in?" wondered Sebastian.

"Well, I'm afraid that once the contest is underway and she realizes that I am close to winning – I am going to win, you know – she'll do something to wreck it." Rosy took a deep breath, then outlined her plan.

"Cool," said Gwen.

Jay looked at Sebastian. Sebastian looked at Rosy. Rosy looked at Jay. Gwen looked at the three of them. Then Jay spoke up. "Well, it does go against the hairdresser's code of ethics, but since The Tangerine is closed on Sundays, we wouldn't technically be there as employees.

"Cool," said Gwen.

Rosy handed out Life Savers, then promised she would find a way to make up their expenses.

"Not necessary," replied Jay. "We've got lots of old stuff kicking around that should be used up."

"Cool," said Gwen.

Soon after Jay and Sebastian left, Rosy had another visitor – her brother John. He had something in a bag, and Rosy could tell by the expression on his face that it wasn't a sack of sandwiches from her mother.

"Hi, Rosy," he muttered, looking anxiously around the room. "Are we alone?"

"Sure," she said. "Gwen's gone for X rays. So what's up?"

"Well…"

"Well what?"

"Well, I want to give you your birthday present." He handed her the bag. "Sorry it's a bit late, but I didn't have a chance to…uh…buy it…until now."

Inside was a brand new copy of *Anne of Green Gables*, and it looked expensive because it was not a paperback. She held it in her hands for a few seconds, then shoved it back into the bag.

"John," she asked, "where did you get the money for this?"

"Look, Rosy," was his answer, "just be happy that you have

the book and now you don't have to worry about getting out of here in time for the contest." His voice cracked. "Now you don't have to go up in front of everyone and…and be a Native Anne."

"John," said Rosy, "I know what you did." She looked into the bag again. "Believe me, the thought has crossed my mind before. But if you get caught, it could affect the whole family. It could hurt Ben's chances at school, and Mom could lose her job. And what if Mom saw the book in my room? With her eagle eyes, there's no way she wouldn't spot it."

"You were there when Mom almost took those cheese slices, Rosy."

"That was different. The lady at the cash register missed scanning the package. That's not the same thing at all. And besides, Mom pointed out her mistake."

"She thought about not saying anything," said John, and Rosy knew he was right.

"Anyway," sighed Rosy, "you'd never feel right about yourself again. And nothing – nothing is worth that."

Rosy tried to think of a way to return the book without anyone finding out.

"John, you've got to get this back into the store right away, and you've got to be careful. Here's how you're going to do it." Rosy told him to carry an armload of library books with him into the store, with the book hidden in the middle of them, and when no one was looking, jam it back on the shelf.

"Any shelf will do," she added. "Don't try to get it back in the right place or they might see you." She handed her brother the book, then grabbed his arm.

"John," said Rosy, "thank you." She felt tears welling up in her eyes. "It means a lot that you would do this for me."

By Friday morning, Dr. Levy had the results from Rosy's tests taken earlier in the week.

They weren't what she'd hoped for at all.

"I'm sorry, Rosy," said the doctor, "but you really need to continue to receive the steroids intravenously."

"Oh, Dr. Levy…you've got to let me go," begged Rosy. "Please let me go on Sunday."

"Rosy, when you were admitted to hospital, you were cyanotic. Your lips were blue." The doctor sat down on the edge of the bed. "Your lung function has not recovered to the point it needs to be."

"But you're going to have to release me eventually." She stopped. *I can't stay here forever*, she thought. *Oh, there are advantages to me being here, for sure. Mom has one less mouth to feed at our place, which takes a load off her.*

Rosy looked out the window, then spoke up. "You know

as well as I do, that I have to go back into that city smog one of these days – and yes, I'm going to have another attack. At least, if you let me out now, I'll get a chance to go out into the country and breathe clean air for a few hours."

"Oh, Rosy," replied the doctor. "You are determined, aren't you?" She said nothing for a full minute. "Okay, I'm going to have a lung specialist go over your tests. He may be able to recommend a stronger oral medication for you. I'm not making any promises, though."

"Thank you, Dr. Levy," said Rosy quietly.

Rosy was released on Saturday at noon, under the condition that she rest in her own bed at home until the contest and return to the hospital as an outpatient on Monday.

Gwen managed three entire words as Rosy was leaving – "Break a leg" – and Rosy appreciated the old stage phrase that really meant good luck. She went to say, "you too," but both of Gwen's legs were already fractured.

Gwen had written down Rosy's phone number several times, and the two would keep in touch. Having made the switch from the afternoon soaps to Rosy's contest, she couldn't stand the idea of not finding out how the whole thing ended.

Finally, it was the night before the day for which Rosy had waited an eternity. And after a week in hospital, she had some time alone – alone with her own thoughts. While the steel mills spewed out smoke into the late-summer sky, a sky otherwise studded with shimmering stars and a big smiling moon, Rosy lay in her little room, with her hand-sewn, ugly yellowish-gray dress and red wig carefully set out, ready for morning.

As she drifted off to sleep, she thought about what Ben had said about their father. That maybe he regretted not getting to know her.

She wondered if he would have come to the contest – if he'd been around. But she knew he wouldn't. He only cared about himself. She hoped she wasn't too much like him.

Chapter 15

Rosy's day was off to a good start. It was sunny and quite warm for the first of September, and she was thinking how great it was going to be to have her own boxed set of books to read in bed on crisp autumn nights.

She took a damp rag and cleaned off her nightstand. It had a drawer in the top and two shelves underneath. Robin bought it at a garage sale, painted it white, and lined it with soft green shelf paper for Rosy. Her discarded copy of *Anne* appeared lonely on the upper shelf, but soon it would have company!

Just before eleven o'clock, Rosy put on her costume and wig, and with carpetbag in hand, came downstairs to the hysterical laughter of Patrick and John (who had safely returned the book), the admiration of Ben, and the sheer pride of Robin, who was amazed that her daughter had enough self-esteem to enable her, as a Native Canadian, to face a crowd of people as Anne of Green Gables. It took guts, and Robin knew it. But she also knew how Rosy got those guts; smooth seas do not a skillful sailor make. It was hardship that had earned her that self-respect, and today was her day to show the world. Robin wouldn't miss it. And, to the delight of Rosy, she put on her best dress: the turquoise one with navy blue flowers.

"Okay, you guys," yelled Rosy, "I've got to get going. Let's load up the Pontiac!"

"Where are your shoes, Rosy?" wondered John.

"I'm going barefoot," was her answer. "It's more convincing."

"You put your shoes on until we get there, Rosy. And where's your inhaler?" Her mother worried that the excitement could easily trigger another attack.

"Right in here." Rosy opened up the carpetbag. "And Mom," she added, sensing Robin's anxiety about her early release from hospital, "I am feeling much better on the new medication. Really."

When Robin, Rosy, and the three boys crossed the street, they found Mr. Spinelli in the front seat with the car started and Mrs. Spinelli beside him. When they saw the Taylors standing there, Mr. Spinelli hollered (over the racket of the radio), "Well, what are you waiting for? Get in! Get in!"

"But I thought we were *borrowing* your car, Mr. Spinelli," Rosy said impatiently. She couldn't remind him with Mrs. Spinelli there that she'd spent three days painting so Ben could take her family to Rockton. "That was our *deal*, right?"

"I said I'd get you to Rockwood, and I'll get you to Rockwood. My wife, she said she wants a ride in the country, so she'll get a ride in the country!" He was still trying to beat the radio. So with Robin, Ben, John, and Patrick jammed in the back seat, and Rosy placed between the Spinellis, off they went down King Street. Mrs. Spinelli had to sit next to the window because she gets carsick. John held on tight to the back door that falls off a lot. Other than driving up over the curb a few times, and narrowly missing a jogger when he was too busy arguing with his wife, Mr. Spinelli managed to get through the downtown area without incident.

It wasn't until they were making their way down Highway 8 that things went wrong. Maybe it was the weight of all the people in the car, maybe it was because the Pontiac wasn't used to going so fast, or maybe it was the fact Mr. Spinelli had patched up the old radiator hose and water pump.

Maybe it was just ordinary bad luck.

But as he rounded the bend outside of Dundas, the engine exploded; and when the engine exploded, Mr. Spinelli threw his arms into the air; and when he threw his arms into the air, the car rolled straight into the ditch.

The steering wheel dropped off, both rear tires went flat, the windshield caved in (except where the duct tape was), the door John tried valiantly to hold on to was lost back where they first went off the road, the entire front section was lodged in the grass, and huge amounts of steam, smoke and fire were shooting out of the hood. The radio continued to work perfectly, though.

With Italian opera music playing at 120 decibels, and Mr. Spinelli shouting at about 140 decibels (which can cause permanent hearing loss in one minute, twenty-nine seconds), it didn't take long before an officer pulled up on a motorcycle. He made sure everyone was all right – they were, except for Rosy, who was fuming more than the front end – and then asked Mr. Spinelli if he had insurance on his car.

"Not much! I can't afford much insurance!" He threw himself against the wreck in a fit of despair. "My car! It's finished this time!"

Then Mrs. Spinelli got her purse out of the steaming front seat, and handed the officer a certificate.

He read it over and said calmly, "Well, I think everything is in order here. It looks like your policy should cover all your expenses, and you'll be able to find yourself another vehicle very soon, I'm sure. If you want, I'll call your broker, and they'll send out a rental car for you. May be a few hours before it gets here, though."

Mr. Spinelli picked himself up. He looked altogether puzzled. He was speechless, for once. His wife was not.

"You've got lots of insurance! I've been paying for it for thirty years! What? You think I'd let you drive around like a maniac with not enough insurance?"

Mr. Spinelli couldn't believe his ears. He grabbed his wife and threw her up in the air. "Lucia! You know what you are? You're an angel from heaven!" He beamed. "Why didn't you tell me?"

"Because it was the only way to keep you from speeding around like a racing car driver! It was the only way I could be sure you'd drive sensibly." She put the certificate back into her purse.

"And you didn't want me to kill myself because you love me. *Bellisima*…Lucia." He planted a big kiss on her cheek.

"You're right! I don't want you to kill yourself. When you get killed, *I'm* going to be the one to do it!" roared Mrs. Spinelli.

In all the excitement, no one noticed that Rosy had

disappeared. Then Robin asked Patrick where she'd gone, and he pointed up the road. She was trying to make a sign out of a piece of old cardboard she picked up from the ditch and lipstick from Robin's purse. It read "**Rockton or Bust!**"

"Rosy! Rosy Taylor!" yelled Robin. "You get right back here this minute, and I mean it. You can't hitchhike!" She ran after her and dragged her back.

Rosy turned to the cop. "Sir, can I have a ride on the back of your motorcycle to Rockton? It's not very far from here, and you see, I'm in this Anne of Green Gables look-alike contest, and I've gone to such great lengths to get this far. I've painted a fence, filled perfume bottles, vacuumed and dusted, spent a week in hospital and a lot of time with a Virgo, who *was* my Plan B for a ride, but who is probably already at the village by now. To be stopped because of a ditched car would be too much for me to take, Sir."

"Oh, Rosy," said Robin, "put a sock in it."

Patrick was busy examining the cop's Harley, John was trying to salvage parts from the Pontiac, and Ben was making sure no one had whiplash. The cop was writing stuff down in a book.

"I guess I need wings to get there!" declared Rosy.

"Wings! That's it!" said Ben, his voice full of excitement. "We need Wing's delivery car!" He asked the officer if he would please call Mr. Wing, who had a cell phone with him at all times. Before Rosy could say chow mein, Mr. Wing was on the line and on his way to pick them up – along with a few skids of bean sprouts, but that didn't matter. He was on his way, and Rosy would soon be on her way to Rockton.

Chapter 16

Mr. Wing pulled up behind the smoldering Pontiac and cheerily greeted the not-so-cheery group (other than Mr. Spinelli who was busy flagging down cars and telling complete strangers about his good fortune).

The Chinese food delivery car was tiny – not a big old clunker like the Pontiac. Even without Mr. and Mrs. Spinelli, who had to wait for the rental to arrive, it would take a lot of squishing to fit two adults, one lanky teenager, three kids, and seven trays of bean sprouts into a hybrid car.

It was decided, after a few tries with different combinations, that Robin and Ben would sit in the front with Mr. Wing, and the three kids would stay in the back, each holding a couple of trays of sprouts. (Rosy didn't care if she had to ride sidesaddle atop the giant egg roll on the roof.)

With the joyous cries of Mr. Spinelli's "*Buona fortuna*! Good luck, Rosa!" fading off into the distance behind them, the Taylors made it to Westfield Heritage Village in one piece. Rosy told Mr. Wing how much she appreciated him driving her to the contest. He claimed he was happy to do so; he was interested in impersonations. He'd noticed that the turnout for his show at the urban mission center had been growing by leaps and bounds each year, and he was now considering pursuing the Elvis thing professionally.

Mr. Wing parked in the shade, so the sprouts didn't turn brown, and pried everyone out of the car. Rosy took a deep breath of country air and checked out the village. There were heritage houses, a general store, a sawmill, an apothecary; she could see why they filmed the *Anne* movie there. The Bright River train station was off to the side. It was exactly like she'd pictured it when she read the book, with its long, wooden platform and white board-and-batten construction.

As they were heading to the station, Rosy saw a taxi pull up with Lydia inside. But it wasn't her at all – it was Anne of Green Gables in the flesh. The custom-made costume, the hair (her own hair, braided neatly), the enormous green eyes that were too big for her face, and the pallid complexion all added up to make an Anne right out of the pages of L. M. Montgomery's book.

She hadn't gone for the yellowish-gray wincey like Rosy (and Mrs. Rodrigues had done a remarkable job given the fact she only had old curtains to work with). Lydia's outfit was obviously something Anne would have worn toward the end of the book, but it was not at all like the stereotypical costumes the other contestants were wearing. It was a simple, loose-fitting dress, exactly right for the time period, and had a blouse underneath made of an antique lilac fabric. It was incredibly authentic, and sure to be appreciated by the judges. Tiffany must have paid a mint for it.

But Rosy knew *she* would win. She would definitely win.

"Hurry up, Lydia!" hollered Rosy. "We've got to get moving! Where have you been? And where's your dad?"

Lydia's face said it all. Once she was close enough, Rosy could tell Lydia had been crying, as her eyes were completely bloodshot and there were red splotches all around her nose. She looked dreadful. "He had an emergency at the hospital. He's not coming. I wasn't going to come either, but the housekeeper called a taxi and threw me in it. So here I am."

"Well, good for Mrs. Harmon," declared Rosy.

"Mrs. Chekhov."

"Okay, good for Mrs. Chekhov," said Rosy. She thought back to how humiliated Lydia had been that day at the hospital. "Lydia, I'm sorry about your dad and everything, but...but..." Once again, Rosy couldn't think of what to say. She had her family, while Lydia stood there heartbroken and alone.

"We'd better get over there," insisted Rosy. "We want to get a good place in line."

Lydia shrugged.

"You've sent in your registration form, haven't you?" asked Rosy.

Lydia nodded.

Robin and the boys came over to say hello.

"Isn't this place great?" Ben pointed out the different buildings. "Look at that bandstand!"

"That's a gazebo," argued John.

As Rosy turned to look, she saw Jay and Sebastian running toward her. They'd driven out on their scooter at full tilt.

"Is she here yet?" gasped Jay, his eyes scouring the crowd frantically.

Lydia, Robin, and the boys didn't know what he was talking about. But Rosy did.

"Oh no," she sighed. "What happened?" She raised an eyebrow as if to ask, "what went wrong with our plan?"

"What's going on here?" questioned Robin.

"The orange stripes...uh, highlights...were an honest mistake," explained Jay. "Tiffany was half an hour late, and the developer sat too long in the dish. Period. Our strategy was to delay her, that's all."

Sebastian crossed his arms in front of his chest. "We could have corrected the problem, but Matilda came into the salon unexpectedly. She happened to mention Rosy and asked if she wanted more work. That's when Tiffany realized that Jay and I knew you, and that's when she put two and two together..."

"And she took off out of the salon," said Jay. "We figured she'd be here by now."

"Are you guys in trouble?" Rosy was worried.

"You could say that," said Jay, drawing a long breath. "We've been fired."

"Fired? Oh no!" Rosy was horrified. What had she done to her friends?

"Fired," said Sebastian, resigning himself to the fact.

"Rosy!" exclaimed a shocked Robin, "I can't believe you had something to do with this."

"Don't be upset, Robin." Jay put his arm around Rosy. "Seb and I have been thinking this may be the best thing that ever happened."

"That's for sure," added Sebastian. "We've been dragging

our feet for years now about starting our own salon, and we're sick of working for Matilda. The wages are terrible, and she takes such a whopping profit, there isn't much left for us."

"And wouldn't clients from The Tangerine come to you guys anyway?" asked Rosy, hoping she was right.

"That's what we're counting on!" Sebastian glanced at his watch. "Shouldn't we be getting over to the train station? I see the girls heading that way. The contest is going to start any time now."

Robin looked at Rosy. "You're still in trouble, young lady. But we'll talk about this later. You've got to concentrate on the contest today. Tomorrow is another story!"

Rosy was relieved that Jay and Sebastian had found the silver lining, and she knew their salon would be a huge success. Lydia, who had been silent, tried to ask Rosy what they'd done to Tiffany, but a man's voice came over the loudspeaker and announced that the contest was about to begin. He told the girls in Rosy's age category to assemble and pick up their nametags at the registration table.

Just as Rosy reached for her tag, she detected a threatening smell – chlorine with a twist of cologne. It was Tiffany. She went straight for Rosy, looking like she'd strangle her with bare hands. Had it not been for her three brothers standing there, she would have.

"It's you! It's you, isn't it? *You're* the one who had my hair ruined." She had a kerchief wrapped around her head. "It's orange!"

"I don't have a clue as to what you're talking about. Now, if you please, I have a contest to get to."

Robin chimed in. "What do you mean speaking to my daughter this way? What does she have to do with your hair…your hair, uh, condition?"

"Oh, you think she's so innocent. She's a troublemaker, that's what she is!" Tiffany went to pull the red wig off Rosy's head, then screamed at the top of her lungs like she was watching a murder take place. "Oh my God! Ahhhhhhhh!" She jumped backward. "Lice!"

Rosy felt the top of her head, found something like a worm and had a look at it.

"It's a bean sprout!" She tossed it into the air and asked Patrick to see if there were any more in there. Then she confronted Tiffany.

"I wasn't going to say anything, but you give me no choice. Now I'll have to tell everyone about your plan."

"What plan?" asked Robin.

"What plan?" asked Ben.

"What plan?" asked Mr. Wing.

"What plan?" asked the woman at the table.

"I'll tell you what plan," blurted Sebastian. "Tiffany

wants to make sure that our Rosy doesn't win!"

"That's right," added Jay.

"What do you have against Rosy?" probed Robin. "She apologized to you."

"Welcome to the Westfield Heritage Village Anne of Green Gables look-alike contest," came the announcer's voice. While he gave a brief history of the village and outlined the rules, the girls gathered in front of the train station. "All entrants must take their place immediately, or be disqualified."

"You're not going anywhere," growled Tiffany, holding Rosy's wrist in a vice-like grip. Years of hockey playing had given her muscles of steel.

"Let me go!" shouted Rosy, "They're going to start without me!"

Rosy's brothers tried to wrench Tiffany off, but Jay had a better idea.

"Look, Seb," he exclaimed, pointing to the other side of the village, "isn't that Sid what's-his-name over there? That famous hockey star? Signing autographs?"

"Where?" shrieked Tiffany, letting Rosy free. "Where did he go?" She made a beeline across the village, and Rosy flew to the stage.

Chapter 17

Lydia followed Rosy up onto the platform but still managed to stumble on the last step. Someone laughed at her. "She's just jealous of your costume," Rosy assured Lydia. She identified a couple of the girls as the ones who had pointed at her during the information session. Rosy tried to ignore them, but they persisted.

"You look stupid in that wig," said the nearest one, as she took her place in line. Then she whispered into her friend's ear (but loud enough so Rosy could hear), "That girl has a lot of nerve entering this contest."

Rosy was glad to be barefoot and dressed in curtains. *At least this time*, she thought, *I'm not wearing anything they might recognize.*

She gazed up and down the row of Anne look-alikes. There were plump Annes, thin Annes, tall Annes, short Annes, pretty Annes, Annes with freckles, Annes without freckles, but she was the only Native Canadian Anne in the lineup. And she was glad. She stood out.

Lydia stood out, too, because of her striking resemblance to L. M. Montgomery's heroine and because of her remarkable costume. There wasn't one other Anne there that even came close. And Lydia could answer questions from the story, too. Rosy was keenly aware that she would have to shine in the talent category to beat Lydia's score.

The first girl recited from the chapter in which Anne gets Diana drunk by mistake. She forgot every other word.

The second girl did the schoolroom scene in which Gilbert Blythe and Anne have a big fight. She kept taking the wig on and off her head to indicate when she was being Anne and when she was being Gilbert. It wouldn't have been so terrible, except she eventually got it mixed up, so when Gilbert called Anne "carrots," *he* was wearing the braids.

The third girl shut down entirely when it was her turn, leaving her friend no choice but to yank her off the stage.

The audience sat through seven more readings, so dull they could be patented as a cure for insomnia. They included four versions of Anne's confession for taking a brooch she didn't take, two of Anne's baking a cake with liniment flavoring, and the unhappy choice of Anne on the ridgepole, during which the unfortunate contestant used the edge of the platform for a roof and tumbled into a bush.

There were several attempts at songs, many of which were completely unrelated to *Anne of Green Gables*. For some reason, one girl sang "Tomorrow" from the musical *Annie* (sorry, but you got the wrong orphan), and another was way out in left field with "Can You Feel the Love Tonight?" from *The Lion King*. No one did.

When Lydia sang "Gee, I'm Glad I'm No One Else but Me," Rosy was prepared for the worst. She hoped it wouldn't be quite as shrill as when she'd sung it at the party, especially given the hours spent with a professional coach, but it was still piercing and had that chalk-on-the-blackboard squeak about it. One rude woman, clearly the mother of an entrant, put a finger in each of her ears to show the judges what she thought.

After Lydia, a girl from Buffalo also sang a song from the musical. And she was excellent. She had a beautiful voice and looked very much like Anne. Her costume wasn't too bad either, and for the first time it dawned on Rosy that someone else could win the contest. That someone else might win those books.

It was that recognition that caused her nerves to flare up and her heart to race. That was the last thing she needed. Dr. Levy had warned her to keep calm.

She picked up her carpetbag, walked to the front of the platform, and faced the crowd directly. Some of them looked like they didn't approve of her.

She didn't care.

She gave the performance of a lifetime.

Rosy looked each member of the audience in the eye and, with every ounce of energy she had, put forth a stunning portrayal of Anne's first words to Matthew, where she describes her life in the asylum and her desire to belong to someone, to anyone.

Everyone, even her competitors, listened intently. She didn't just *recite* the words of L. M. Montgomery, she brought something to the story – something of herself, of her life.

By the time she'd finished, Rosy had made everyone understand what it was to be an orphan with nothing in the world but the clothes on your back. They knew what it was like to have to carry around an old carpetbag with a handle that pulls out if it isn't held in just the right way. And they knew how it felt to finally belong to someone.

When she looked out into the crowd, she saw people wiping their eyes. Their applause was so loud, Rosy figured the Spinellis could hear it from where they were, regardless of the radio.

The judges moved on to the question and answer part of the contest, and both Rosy and Lydia responded to every question correctly. The other girls, including the one from Buffalo, were gradually weeded out by giving wrong or incomplete answers, and then the two finalists were named: Lydia Parker and Rosy Taylor.

Rosy could hear her two younger brothers yelling cheers of congratulations but kept herself centered on the task at hand.

The judges deliberated for several minutes, then announced the tally: Lydia had gained ten points for her costume and resemblance, while Rosy had five, but Lydia had only three points for her song, while Rosy had earned the full ten for her reading.

The score was fifteen to thirteen in Rosy's favor, and the last question was worth three points. If she answered it correctly, which she most certainly would, she would be declared the winner. Rosy was so happy, she could hardly contain herself.

Everyone stood in silence as the two girls heard their final questions. Lydia's was first.

"Can you tell the judges the three things for which Matthew asks in Lawson's store in the twenty-fifth chapter of the book? Please take your time, as any answer you give will be final."

"A rake, hayseed and sugar – um, brown sugar," replied Lydia.

"Correct," announced the judge.

It was time for Rosy's question, and she stepped forward.

"Can you tell the judges the color of the dress with puffed sleeves that Matthew gives Anne in the twenty-fifth chapter of the book? Please take your time, as any answer you give will be final."

The dress with puffed sleeves, thought Rosy, smiling to herself. *Helen will laugh when she hears that the judges asked me this one.*

Just as she was about to give her response, Rosy saw a red sports car pull into the parking lot. She wondered if it was Lydia's father.

It *was* Dr. Parker! He raced toward the train station and to the front of the crowd.

When Lydia spotted him, her eyes filled with tears – only this time, they were tears of joy. Oh, how she wanted to win the competition and make her dad proud. Rosy could see how much she wanted to. How much she *needed* to.

But this was *Rosy's* contest to win. She'd put so much effort into it. So much work. There was no taxi-ride to

Rockton for her. No custom-made costume for her.

Lydia didn't need those books. Or the trophy.

Rosy did.

It was Rosy who was like Anne. It was Rosy who knew what it felt like to have no worldly goods. Lydia had tons of stuff. She might look like Anne, but her life was completely different.

And then Anne's words to Matthew went through Rosy's mind – when she tells him that she'd never really belonged to anyone.

Rosy thought for a minute, then realized it wasn't worldly goods that Anne wanted. What she wanted was to belong to someone. To anyone. And despite everything in Rosy's life – the pollution, the food bank, the secondhand clothes – she belonged. She belonged to her mother, to her brothers, and to her neighborhood.

It was Lydia who felt like she didn't belong to anyone.

It was Lydia who sat alone all day in her pink room. It was Lydia whose housekeepers didn't stick around. It was Lydia whose friends didn't show up for her party. And it was Lydia whose mother was gone with the wind.

It was Lydia who felt like an orphan.

It was Lydia who was just like Anne.

Maybe she did need to win the contest.

Maybe it was Rosy who didn't.

"Your answer, please?" Rosy had kept the judges waiting long enough. She knew what she had to do.

"The dress was…blue."

"I'm sorry, Miss Taylor, that answer is incorrect. The correct answer is brown.

"Miss Lydia Parker, on behalf of the panel, I am delighted to pronounce you the winner of the Westfield Village Anne of Green Gables look-alike contest."

When Dr. Parker cheered and leaped up onto the platform to kiss Lydia, Rosy knew she'd done the right thing.

Maybe she wasn't like her father after all.

She joined her mom and brothers in the audience.

"I'm sorry, Rosy," said Robin, "but you can try again next year, if you want to. Anyway, you came in second, and that is terrific. We're all *really* proud of you."

"Sure," said John, "forget about it. You were the best one up there. That song of Lydia's was enough to make birds drop out of the sky."

Patrick and Ben added their encouraging words, as did Mr. Wing, who suggested she try singing next time.

"Take a bow, Rosy! You were fantastic," declared Jay, and Sebastian agreed.

"So what happened to Tiffany?" wondered Rosy.

"She came back, but when she saw that man with Lydia, she ducked out fast," replied Jay. Then he and Sebastian said their good-byes and headed home to start making plans for their salon.

Lydia hurried to catch up with Rosy.

"You know, I thought the dress was blue, too," she said, out of breath. "I want you to have these." She handed the boxed set of books to Rosy.

"No, Lydia. This is your prize." She couldn't help glancing at the colorful spines and admiring the beautiful artwork on the side of the box. But it didn't belong to her. She tried to give it back to Lydia.

"I won't be happy unless you take them. Don't you remember, Rosy, how Anne felt when Matthew gave her the chocolates? She told Marilla they would taste so much sweeter if she could give half to Diana. Well, my trophy will mean so much more to me if you accept these books. Please."

So Rosy had a boxed set of the whole series – factory sealed and fresh off the press, with the smell of printer's ink still on them. The complete set of eight, never before read by anyone else. Never touched by anyone else. Not sneezed on, not set down on a bus seat, not dropped on the sidewalk.

And not just any set of eight. A set given to her by a kindred spirit.

Chapter 18

Lydia's father joined the group with the trophy under his arm. "Well, you two girls did a fabulous job, taking first and second places."

"Yes, they certainly did," agreed Robin.

"Dad, do we have to leave right away, or can I go over to the store with Rosy?" Lydia wanted to see a bit of the village before going home.

Rosy looked at Mr. Wing. "I'll only be a minute. I know you have to get back to the restaurant." She turned to Lydia and Dr. Parker. "Mr. Wing saved the day. He came all the way out here just to give us a ride."

"It was no problem, Rosy. I enjoyed it."

Then Lydia's father spoke up. "Oh, Ben…it is Ben, isn't

it?" He pulled a paper out of his pocket. "Dr. Levy asked me to give you this phone number. She spoke with someone from the Native Physicians' Association, and it appears you were given the wrong information – the bursary *would* cover all your expenses. And they can help you find a volunteer position, too."

"Hey, that's great!" exclaimed Rosy, giving her brother's arm a squeeze. Ben stood in disbelief that he might be going to university after all.

"My loss will be the medical profession's gain," declared Mr. Wing with a sigh, and everyone laughed.

"Mom," said Rosy, "can you hang on to these for me?" She handed her mom the boxed set of books. "But don't set them down anywhere, okay?"

"I won't," Robin promised. "I won't."

Rosy and Lydia ran ahead and took a look inside the old-fashioned general store.

There was candy for sale at the register. Lydia reached for the Life Savers, but to the surprise of Rosy, her hand went right past the cherry ones and to the butterscotch instead. She opened them up for Rosy to take one. She took two.

"Butterscotch?" asked Rosy. "I figured you'd never get off the red ones!"

"One small step for me," said Lydia resolutely, "one giant leap for Virgos everywhere."

Rosy couldn't resist giving Lydia a hug. "You're the best Virgo I ever met."

In that moment, Rosy recognized something about life. She thought how in the past month, so many things had changed. Mr. Spinelli would soon be in his driveway, washing a brand new used Pontiac; Jay and Sebastian were starting their own business at last; Ben no longer had to deliver Chinese food until he was forty-eight to afford school; and Lydia didn't have to depend on cherry Life Savers anymore.

"You know," she told Lydia, "I've heard it said that life is something that happens to you while you're busy making other plans."

And when she realized what a good friend she had found in Lydia, she knew it was true.

Caroline Stellings is an artist, author, and children's book illustrator. She loves to write and paint the birds and animals that frequent the wetland area just outside the windows of her home studio. Her previous books for children include the popular *Skippers at Cape Spear*. Caroline lives in the small town of Waterdown near Hamilton, Ontario.